P9-DWP-934

Grand County Middle School
MEDIA CENTER
Moab, Utah 84532

LEXILE 680 LEVEL 9-12 POINTS

MOONKIND

Sarah Prineas

MOONKIND

HARPER

An Imprint of HarperCollins*Publishers*

Moonkind

Copyright © 2014 by Sarah Prineas

Moonkind
Copyright © 2014 by Sarah Prineas
All rights reserved. Printed in the United States of America.
No part of this book may be used or reproduced in any manner
whatsoever without written permission except in the case of brief
quotations embodied in critical articles and reviews. For information
address HarperCollins Children's Books, a division of HarperCollins
Publishers, 10 East 53rd Street, New York, NY 10022.
www.harpercollinschildrens.com

Library of Congress Cataloging-in-Publication Data
Prineas, Sarah.
    Moonkind / Sarah Prineas. — First Edition.
        pages   cm
    Sequel to: Summerkin.
    Summary: "Fer, the Lady of the Summerlands, trusted the Lords
and Ladies of her world to fulfill their oaths by removing their glamories, but their pledges have gone forsworn, and now the consequences
of their broken promises are ravaging the land and it's up to Fer to
restore peace before it's too late"— Provided by publisher.
    ISBN 978-0-06-192109-4 (hardback)
    [1. Magic—Fiction.   2. Shape-shifting—Fiction.   3. Fantasy.]
I. Title.
PZ7.P93646Moo 2013   2013032167
[Fic]—dc23   CIP
                                                        AC

Typography by Andrea Vandergrift
14 15 16 17   CG/RRDH   10 9 8 7 6 5 4 3 2
❖
First Edition

*To Deb Coates, who taught me that dog reasons
are not our reasons. Also to her dog, Blue,
who thinks about rabbits even more than Rook does.*

prologue

Under a full moon, four black horses raced over the hills, their hooves drumming on the grass, their flame-colored eyes flashing. The leader, a tall horse whose mane was braided and knotted with glinting crystals, swerved, finding a new course, and the rest of the horses swerved too and galloped on, following.

Pucks, all of them.

Three of the pucks raced along, reveling in their strength, in the stretch of muscles moving under a smooth coat, in their strong bond with one another, and in the wind blowing through their manes. They were running toward trouble and chaos and fun, and the whole reason for being a puck.

The fourth puck felt all that, but he felt something else, too.

He was a puck, and as a puck he should be true only to his brother-pucks and nobody else. But he had a thread, the merest fragile spider-silk thread, tying his heart to another heart far away. He wasn't sure what the thread was, exactly. It was just there, and somehow he didn't quite want to break it, though breaking it would be as easy as taking a breath and letting it out again. So on he ran, free and wild with his brothers, but feeling at the same time the faintest pull toward something else.

Ahead was a forest, dark and thick with pine trees. As they drew near it, the horses slowed. The air around them blurred, and one by one they changed from horse to person-shaped for just a moment, and then another swift, blurring change into dog. And now a small pack of black-furred, yellow-eyed dogs ran shoulder to shoulder through the dark, piney woods.

They flowed like a furry, black river over fallen trunks and piles of stone, winding through the close-growing trees. Above them the wind raced too, making a *rush-rush-rush* sound in the high branches.

At last the four dogs came to a mossy clearing. They spat out their shifter-tooths and stood panting in their person shapes again. The moon hung directly over the clearing, casting sharp shadows.

"Is this it?" one of the pucks asked. For clothes he wore a wrap made of tattered, yellow silk.

The second puck, this one wearing nothing but red and black paint, answered. His eyes glinted with a redder flame than his brother-pucks' did. "It is," he growled. "Quiet."

The third puck, the leader with the long braids woven with shiny bits, glanced up at the moon. "Any moment now, and the Way here will open." He nodded at the painted puck. "It's going to be a wonderful trick, this."

The painted puck barked out a laugh. "This is maybe the best puck-plan ever made, brothers. It'll turn everything upside down."

The leader glanced aside at the fourth puck, the youngest of them all. The one with the strange heart-thread that they all knew about but didn't understand. "You're with us, Rook?"

The puck called Rook wore ragged shorts and had bare feet. Old scars traced like jagged, white lines across his chest and one shoulder. He stood a little separate from his brothers as if he was with them, but not *quite* the same as they were.

The other pucks watched, their yellow eyes shining, and waited to hear what Rook would say.

"Well, Brother?" the leader puck asked.

In answer, Rook nodded. Then he grinned. "I am with you, yes," he said. "Let's go."

one

The girl named Fer lay on her back in her grandmother's
yard gazing up at the full moon. Here in the human world,
the wheel of the seasons had turned again while she'd been
gone, and time had flowed away, and shy spring was edging out from behind winter's shadow. Fer felt the chill of
cold dirt underneath her back; dry grass prickled against
her bare arms. She shivered. In a moment she'd go in and
see Grand-Jane, but she needed more time outside first.

The moon, the moon. In her own land, the Summerlands, the moon was full too, but there the summer was
turning brittle with the coming of fall.

"Is that you, Jennifer?" came Grand-Jane's voice from
the direction of the house.

Fer turned her head. Her grandma was standing on

the bottom of the steps leading to the kitchen door. In the darkness she was mostly a shadow wrapped in a knitted sweater, but the moon gleamed in her hair, making it glow white.

Was Grand-Jane's hair whiter than it had been before? Did her face look more tired? Fer wasn't sure. It was hard to remember, when time passed so quickly here and so slowly in the Summerlands.

"Yes, it's me," Fer answered. "I'll be right there."

The sky wasn't as dark here as it was in the Summerlands. Here the lights from town meant the stars never seemed close enough to touch and the moon's beams were not so pure a silver.

Fer's place was through the Way, but something always drew her back to Grand-Jane. Love, of course—that was part of it. Maybe she also needed the reminder that she was human—partly human, anyway—and still a girl even though she was supposed to be a wise and noble Lady of her land too. Sometimes being both of those things was confusing. Some of what had happened was confusing, too, and a little frightening. She'd spent the summer tending to her land and trying to decide if she'd made a huge mistake. Talking to Grand-Jane about it would make everything clearer.

"Are you going to come in?" came Grand-Jane's voice from the steps.

If she wanted Grand-Jane's advice she'd have to go into the house. But it made her twitchy, being closed inside a roof and walls.

"Now, my girl," Grand-Jane insisted.

Fer pushed herself up and stood, the ground cold under her bare feet. At the kitchen door, Grand-Jane opened her arms and Fer came into them, putting her head on her grandma's shoulder. For that one second she was just a girl and didn't have to make any hard decisions or be noble or brave. She took a deep, shuddering breath.

"All right," Grand-Jane said softly. She dropped a quick kiss on Fer's forehead and then held her at arm's length, inspecting her. "You look tired."

"A lot has happened," Fer said.

"Well." Grand-Jane frowned. "Come inside and tell me about it." She went into the kitchen, crossing to the counter, where she put the kettle on the stove and turned it on. "What happened to the puck?" she asked.

"Oh, Rook," Fer said with a sigh, and leaned against the door frame. "He's gone off with his brothers."

"Is he your friend?" Grand-Jane asked.

"I don't know," Fer answered. He'd almost betrayed her. She wanted to think of him as a friend, but every time she felt as if a bond of friendship had formed between them, he reminded her that he was a puck. To him, being a puck meant never being friends with a Lady like her. "He might be my friend, and he might not."

"You'll have to decide one way or another," Grand-Jane said. "Now tell me the rest of it."

Where to start? "I had to prove that I am the true Lady of the Summerlands," Fer said slowly.

"Prove?" Grand-Jane asked, turning from the counter with her eyebrows raised. "You either are or you aren't."

Fer shrugged. "They didn't like that I'm partly human. There was a contest. I lost every part of it but . . ." She shook her head. "I won in the end." She'd won because of her human-ness, she knew, which was funny when she thought about it. "I'm the true Lady now, and I swore an oath to serve the land and the people."

"Usually it works the other way, I think," Grand-Jane said.

"Yes," Fer said. "Usually the people swear oaths to their Lords or Ladies." She didn't like oaths. They were a giant, knotty problem that she hadn't figured out yet. She edged farther into the kitchen. "At the end of everything some Lords and Ladies and their leader, who's named Arenthiel, invaded my lands. I defeated them—well, not just me, but all of us, and the pucks too—and I made them swear to take off their glamories and stop ruling their lands and their people."

"*You* made *them* swear an oath?" Grand-Jane asked.

She had stopped making tea and was leaning against the counter, listening.

Fer nodded, and her stomach gave a lurch. "I had to. The glamories are really bad."

"Hmm." Grand-Jane turned back to the counter; she plucked a few leaves off a marjoram plant on the windowsill and added them to the teapot. "I know the word *glamour*, but I don't think I understand what a glamorie is."

Fer had worn a glamorie twice, but she wasn't sure she understood either. "Well, it makes the person who puts it on look beautiful." That was one thing. "And if you give a command when you're wearing it, people have to obey." She hadn't liked that part. And there was another thing. "It does something to the person wearing it too." She thought back to the one long night she'd worn the glamorie—how it'd turned her thoughts icy cold and uncaring. "It made me feel frozen," she finished.

Grand-Jane added boiling water to the teapot and brought it to the table. "And all the Lords and Ladies of the lands through the Way wear one of these things?" she asked.

"Most of them," Fer said.

"And you think they should take the glamories off," Grand-Jane said, setting out a mug. "Come and have some tea."

Fer stepped farther into the kitchen. Being in the house *really* made her twitchy.

"It's rosemary and lavender, with some marjoram for remembrance," Grand-Jane added, stirring in a spoonful of honey made by her own bees. "There, nice and sweet." She pushed the mug across the table, toward Fer.

"Thanks," Fer said, and slipped into a chair. To make Grand-Jane happy, she could stay inside for a little while. It wasn't so awful. She went back to her grandma's question. "Um, yes." She took a sip of hot tea. "It's bad that the Lords and Ladies are wearing the glamories. They're connected to their lands, just like I am. They don't really need the glamories. It's not good for anybody. The glamories give them power they haven't earned, and it makes them rule their lands and people, instead of loving them and helping them."

"You've brought changes to those lands," her grandma said.

Fer nodded. Yes, she had.

Grand-Jane took a sip of tea. "They won't like it."

"I know," Fer answered. She stayed quiet for a moment. "What do you think I should do?"

Grand-Jane frowned down at her tea. When she spoke, her voice was low. "Jennifer, the first time I let you go through the Way, I knew I was sending you into danger. I knew you had to go then, and I know you have to go back now. . . ." Her voice trailed off. Then her grandma took a deep breath as if she'd decided something. She looked up at Fer. "You demanded that those Lords and Ladies remove their glamories. You bound them to an oath that they might not be willing to fulfill. Now you have to deal with the consequences of that."

Fer nodded. The girl part of her felt a little shivery at what Grand-Jane was asking her to do—to *deal with consequences*—but the Lady part of her knew her grandma was right. If the Lords and Ladies weren't willing to abide by the oath they had sworn, bad things would happen unless Fer forced them, somehow, to fulfill their oaths.

That *somehow* was the problem.

They sat quietly and sipped tea for a while.

Fer felt the ceiling pressing down on her like a giant hand. Being away from her land made it feel like she had a gaping hole in her chest where her heart should be. The Summerlands pulled at her. So did the things she had to *deal with*. "Grand-Jane," she started, jumping to her feet.

Grand-Jane sighed and set down her mug. "I know." She got up and came around the table, where she pulled Fer into a hug. "You can't stay."

"I'm sorry," Fer mumbled into Grand-Jane's shoulder. She felt her grandma kiss her temple.

Then Grand-Jane pushed her toward the door and turned away. "Remember, my girl," she said in a brisker voice, her back to Fer. "Remember that part of you is still human."

"I don't ever forget it," Fer said.

"See that you don't. And it sounds like you've stirred up some dangerous things over there. Be careful."

"I will," Fer said. She went to the door and opened it. The chill night air rolled in. On the doorstep she paused. Grand-Jane was all alone here. She'd been alone all the long, cold winter. "Will you come with me?" she asked. "Through the Way?" She'd asked once before, and her grandma had said no. But maybe this time . . .

"My place is here, Jennifer," Grand-Jane said quietly. Fer heard her take a deep breath. "Next time, just don't wait so long to come see me."

"I won't," Fer promised—the kind of promise that couldn't be broken. "I'll come again soon." And then she flung herself out into the night.

two

Phouka was waiting on the other side of the Way. As Fer stepped into the moonlit clearing, her connection to the Summerlands swept through her. Every Lord and Lady of every land had such a connection to their lands. She didn't know what it was like for those others, but it made her tingle with awareness of her land from the top of her head to the soles of her bare feet. She was rooted here, deeper than any tree.

Home.

Still, she felt a little nagging worry. *Be careful,* her grandma had warned, and she was right to warn. The lands were beautiful and magical, and she belonged here for sure—but Fer was part human, which meant she brought change. And change wasn't all that welcome.

Phouka whickered and she leaned against him,

patting his neck, smelling the warm-grass smell of horse, feeling the warmth of his coat under her hands. "Hello, you bad horse," she said, smiling. The people of the Summerlands—of all the lands—were people, but they each had a connection to a kind of animal or plant, and something of the spirit of that animal or plant inside themselves. Phouka was different. He'd been a puck like Rook, but he'd been stuck in his horse form for as long as she'd known him. Unlike his puck-brother Rook, he was trustworthy—a true friend.

She closed her eyes. Hmm. The land felt peaceful under the full moon. She felt the fall creeping in, the trees pulling in the sap from their leaves, the animals hurrying to gather food and grow thicker pelts for the long, icy winter nights. Before she left, she'd been keeping one thread of awareness on a corner of the forest where some bark-borer beetles had been spreading from one tree to another, but it seemed all right. The trees were holding their own. Anyway, as she'd learned, a few fallen trees weren't a bad thing. With all the bugs and worms and mushrooms that moved in, there was more life in a rotting log than in a living tree.

She felt a tug on one of the threads that tied her to the people of the land—while she'd been gone, a badger-man had fallen sick with a cough. She'd have to check on him soon.

Keeping her eyes closed, she checked for something

else. From her time dealing with the Mór, she knew that a broken oath left a kind of stain on the land. With all her mind, she searched her land for any taint, anything that might hint that the oaths she'd demanded had gone wrong.

There was nothing. Everything was as it should be.

As she opened her eyes, a sudden breeze leaped up, and the trees that edged the clearing around the Way bowed and shivered. A few brown leaves ripped from their branches and shredded away in the wind. Rags of cloud dashed across the moon. The night darkened.

Fer felt the wild wind blowing through her, too. "Let's ride!" she shouted to Phouka.

In answer, he snorted and tossed his head, and she swung herself onto his back. She'd hardly gotten a grip on his mane when he was off, pounding down the path through the dark forest. The wind raced along with them, and the tree branches thrashed as they passed. "Faster!" she shouted, and Phouka neighed like laughing, and stretched into his fastest run.

Fer crouched over his neck and clung to his mane with all her strength. Their speed blew tears from her eyes and she blinked them away. She couldn't see what was ahead; the path was all moon-silvered shadows. A twig snagged her head and she felt the tie come off the end of her braid, and her hair unraveled into a tangled banner that waved behind her as they flew. Down the path they went, faster and faster, and for just a second Fer *was* the wind rushing through the dark night.

Then Phouka crashed out of the forest and into the wide clearing that surrounded the Lady Tree, with Fer's house and lots of other little houses perched in its branches along with bridges and ladders down to the ground. Phouka raced around the clearing once more and then slowed into a jolting trot: *bump, bump, bump.*

"Pho-uka, let-me-off," Fer said, trying not to bite her tongue as she spoke.

Phouka tossed his head and bumped her around the clearing a second time.

Fer laughed. He was a puck, after all. Lucky for her, he didn't find a nice big thornbush and toss her into it. Finally he stopped, snorting, and Fer slid off his back. "Oh, very funny," she whispered into his ear, still smiling. Then Phouka's ear twitched and he pushed with his nose on her shoulder, and she turned to see what he was looking at.

In the darkness, a campfire glowed at the base of the Lady Tree with some people standing around it, watching her.

"G'night, Phouka," Fer said with a final pat, and went to see who it was.

As she got closer, she saw the young wolf-guard, Fray,

standing with her burly arms folded, looking fierce in the firelight. Fer nodded, and Fray nodded back. Next to her, Fer saw one tall, pale shape and a second, shorter, darker shape with . . . was it embers burning at the ends of its hair?

It was. What were *they* doing here? "Hello, Lich," Fer said slowly. "Hello, Gnar."

The fire-girl gave Fer a brisk nod. "Hello, Lady Strange," she said. Like when Fer had first met her, Gnar was dressed all in black silk; her skin was the color of burned paper, and so was her hair—except for the coals burning at the end of each long braid.

Beside her, the swamp-boy, Lich, gave a solemn bow. "Lady Gwynnefar." Lich was tall and thin and wore mushroom-colored clothes studded here and there with shiny bits that glimmered like dew.

Gnar and Lich had been her rivals during the competition to win the Summerlands crown. Fer had once felt a flicker of friendship from them, but they'd allied with Arenthiel during his invasion of the Summerlands, so they hadn't been friends after all.

Fer shook her head, confused. "Um, what are you doing here?"

"We were sent," Gnar said with a dry grin. She cast a slanting glance at Lich beside her. "She looks like a wildling thing, doesn't she, Dewdrop?"

Lich nodded. "She does indeed, Spark," he answered.

Fer looked down at herself. Her long hair was tangled and had twigs and bits of leaves snared in it. Her clothes, the shorts and T-shirt she'd been wearing all summer, were pretty much rags, and she had what her grandma would call *dirt socks* on her bare feet.

Well, all right. Maybe she *had* turned a little wild during the long, green days, her first summer of being truly and completely the Lady of this land.

"Speaking of wild, the pucks aren't here, are they, Lady Gwynnefar?" Lich asked. He looked uneasily out at the darkness past the campfire, as if a crowd of pucks was out there waiting to leap on him.

"No, they're not," Fer answered. The pucks came and went as they pleased, but mostly they were off somewhere else. Usually getting into trouble.

"Well, that makes things easier," Gnar said. "We've come from the nathe. Sent by the High Ones."

Fer felt a shiver of worry. The High Ones ruled over all the lands, and the nathe was their palace. She hadn't felt anything amiss in her own land, but if the High Ones had sent messengers . . . something was wrong.

She stepped past Gnar and Lich to the fire. The night air had an edge of frost in it, and the warmth from the flames felt good against her bare legs. Overhead in the Lady Tree, the Lady's bees, whose buzzing speech only she could understand, hovered in a sleepy cloud. The rest of the land's people, she sensed, were asleep.

"All well, Ladyfer?" Fray asked quietly. That's what the people of the Summerlands called her now—*Ladyfer*. It was better than *Lady Gwynnefar*, anyway.

"I hope so, Fray," Fer answered, and held her hands up to warm them.

Lich and Gnar joined her. Gnar stood so close to the fire, she was practically in the flames. Lich stood a few steps back, and Fer saw steam rising up around him. "What do the High Ones want?" Fer asked.

"They ask you to come to the nathe, Lady Gwynne-far," Lich answered.

"The High Ones don't show it," Gnar said, "but we know they are worried. You started something."

"A change," Lich put in.

Gnar nodded. "A change, yes. And now you need to see it through." The fire-girl leaned closer, and Fer saw the flames deep in her eyes. "They want to speak with you. They won't force you to leave your land, but you need to come. Will you, Lady? Will you come?"

three

This Way was open only at midnight and for a short time after that; at all other times it was closed, like a locked door. Rook caught a glimpse of white teeth flashing in his brother-puck Tatter's dark face as he grinned.

"It's time," Tatter said. "Let's go."

The moonlight shone down and the Way opened. Rook stepped into it with his brothers. Every Way was different; going through this Way felt like being stabbed with daggers made of ice. He was shivering by the time he stumbled out the other side.

"All right, Pup?" Asher asked.

His teeth chattering, Rook nodded. His brothers had a plan. They hadn't told him exactly what it was, but it would bring trouble to those who deserved it, so he would help them see it through.

He stepped up to stand shoulder to shoulder with his brothers, surveying the land they'd entered. They stood on bare rock that gleamed under the light of the heavy, low-hanging full moon. The rock was like a plain, seamed here and there with cracks. Nothing grew here, not even lichen. The air felt dry and dead.

"We don't have much time before the Way closes again," Asher said, and in the cold air a cloud of steam puffed out with his words. "Come on. We go toward the moon."

They shifted into their dog shapes and padded over the rock. Rook sniffed with his dog nose, but the air smelled like nothing but dust and chill. After a long run, he saw something gleaming in the distance. As they got closer, he saw a spire of rock like a finger pointing at the moon. The spire was tall—as tall as a pine tree. Spread all around it was something that glistened under the moonlight, like cloth made of diamonds, or silver nets, or like . . .

Spiderwebs?

As his brothers slowed, Rook did too, and then spat out his shifter-tooth, catching it in his hand and stowing it in the pocket of his ragged shorts.

A glittering web stretched from the top of the rock-spire to the ground. In the middle of the web was a huge spider. It was as big as a horse, but the web didn't sag under its weight. Its body was clear, as if it were made of glass. The moon shone into it, Rook saw, and the spider spun out shimmering lengths of thread made of moonlight. The spider's eight legs were long and spindly, and *click-clack*ed as it deftly drew the strands of moonlight out of itself and wove them into its web. All around it, flowing out from the stone spire, more web lapped up to the pucks' feet like a gleaming sea.

It reminded him of something. But *what*?

He must've looked confused. Asher spoke, his voice harsh in the silence. "It's glamorie, Pup."

Rook blinked and looked again. Ash was right. He'd seen web like this before; he'd seen Fer toss it over herself like a silver net, and then he'd seen Fer's wolf-guard and her fox-girl maid bow to her as if she were a queen.

Fer, he knew, hadn't liked that. But the Lords and Ladies of all the other lands—they liked what their glamories did.

"Rip's been spying on some of the Lords and Ladies," Asher said. "Following them. They take a different route here every time, trying to keep it secret, but we figured it out. They come here to harvest the web and cut it into pieces, and then they use it to rule."

Rip glanced aside at him and gave a sharp smile. "They say we pucks are liars and cheats. But they're the ones lying when they wear these webs."

"They are," Rook agreed.

"They'll not give them up," Asher said. The glamories, he meant.

"Not without a fight," Rip agreed.

As an answer, Asher gave a snarling smile. "We'll see about that, brothers. Now, there should be a chasm or a ravine nearby," he said, looking around at the barren rock. "Cast out to search for it."

Each of the pucks set out in a different direction. Rook stayed in his person form, shivering at the cold wind blowing across his shoulders. Leaving the moonspinner spider behind, with the rising moon low in the sky on his right, he searched. He walked for a long time. The only sound was the hiss of the wind over the bare rock. The moonlight shone down, sheeny white. There was nothing here; Rook felt sure. This land was empty, except for the spider.

But no, wait. Ahead was something else. He crept closer, staying low and quiet, the rock cold under his bare feet. A wide crack in the rock that looked like it was sucking in the light, leaving only darkness. This was it, what his brothers had come here to find.

Rook glanced over his shoulder. He'd walked a long way; the spire stuck up in the distance, the spider there only a bright spot in the night. He saw movement on the rock plain: his brother-pucks, searching. "Here!" Rook shouted and waved, and he thought he saw a wave in return.

He turned back to the chasm. Might as well take a look while he waited. The moon had crept higher into the sky, so he could see well enough. Carefully he edged up to the jagged rim of the crack in the rock and knelt to look in. The chasm was far too wide to leap across, and it was deep and full of sharp shadows cast by the slanting moonlight. He could see a narrow path leading down to a ledge. Below that was only darkness, but he thought he saw something moving down there too.

The path wasn't much of a path. He had to go sideways down it, his chest scraping on the rock wall of the chasm, his feet feeling their way. Down and down he went, deeper and deeper, until he got to a ledge. He stepped off the path and crouched. A foul smell drifted up from below. His nose wrinkled. It was the smell of rotting offal and swamp and dead fish—a stench so heavy and oily, it almost seemed to cling to his skin. *Something* had to be down there, making that smell. He lay on his chest on the ledge, peering into the roiling darkness.

A thin voice called from above. "Pup, are you there?"

He was about to answer, *I am, yes*, when the ledge crumbled away beneath him and he was sliding down a steep slope in a tumble of rocks. With a yell and a splash he landed in something as cold and thick as mud, but slick with the horrible smell too.

At that moment, the moon rose high enough in the sky to peek over the edge of the chasm. Its light shone down, and Rook saw that the bottom of the chasm was a cesspit full of stinking, bubbling muck, and there were *things* moving in the shadows. Things with *eyes*. He scrambled to his feet and backed away, beslimed with muck. With his hands he felt for a crack in the wall so he could climb away.

The things in the darkness came closer. He heard a sucking sound like something big dragging itself through mud, and then a huge spider lurched into a shaft of the pale moonlight. It was the twin of the moon-spinner spider, but instead of glass and moonlight, it was dank black and stuffed with darkness. It dragged a rotting, clotted mess of a web behind it. More clots of web clung to the walls of the chasm. Fat baby spiders the size of Rook's hand skittered over the surface of the mud, or clung to the muck-spider's spindly legs, or darted forward to examine Rook and then scuttle away.

"Ash!" he shouted desperately, his back to the wall. *Get me out of here!* He gasped for breath, and the heavy, stinking air caught his throat, making him choke and cough.

"Pup!" he heard from just above him.

"Careful!" he croaked back. "The ledge is crumbling away."

He heard the sound of urgent voices, whispering.

Come on, brothers.

The muck-spider lurched closer.

"Hurry!" he shouted, and his voice echoed off the steep walls of the ravine.

A long, spindly spider leg dripping with muck probed toward him. It had a knife-edged pincer on its end that went *snap, snap, snap.* He edged away and slipped, and as he went down into the muck, he felt something slimy brush against his hand and then cling, as if it was set with tiny barbs. Coughing, he scrambled to his feet again. The spider moved closer, and he heard its mouthparts moving, a scraping, gurgling sound. It wasn't going to *eat* him, was it?

"Here, Brother," he heard from just above.

Rook looked up. Ash, on the ledge with Tatter behind him, holding his shirt as Ash leaned forward, stretching his arm down.

"Jump for it, Pup," Ash ordered.

With a desperate leap, Rook jumped, grabbing for Ash's hand with the hand not covered with slimy muck. As his brother-puck hoisted him up, Rook heard the snap of pincer-claws closing on air right where he'd been cowering against the chasm wall.

Ash dragged him onto the crumbling ledge. "And on up," Ash said, shoving Rook ahead of him onto the path. He followed Tatter, with Ash right behind, along the path until they reached the top, where Rip was waiting.

Rook crawled off the path and lay flat on the rock, panting.

"You all right, Pup?" Asher asked from where he crouched a few steps away.

Rook jerked out a nod.

"You weren't bitten?" Tatter asked, kneeling beside him. He put a hand on Rook's forehead.

"I wasn't, no," Rook answered. He shoved Tatter's hand aside and sat up. The bit of muck was still stuck to his palm. He scraped it against the rock, but it wouldn't come off.

"Phew, the stink of you!" Asher said, standing next to him now.

Beside him, Rip grinned, and his flame-red eyes flashed. "Should we toss him back in?"

Rook scrambled away from Rip, who was unchancy enough to actually do it. "No!" he gasped. He glanced back at the chasm. "What was that thing?"

"Shadow-spinner spider," Ash answered. "Twin of the moon-spinner back there." He nodded toward the spire in the distance.

Tatter was staring at Rook's hand. "You've got a bit of its web on you."

"It won't come off." He tried scraping it on the rock again.

Ash glanced aside at Rip, who nodded. "No, leave it, Pup. It's what we came here for." Ash looked up at the full moon. "We have time for a test. We'd better hurry, though, so we can get back to the Way before it closes."

At that, Rip grinned. "And then we can get our pup here a bath, can't we?"

"Oh, yes indeed," Tatter said, getting to his feet and backing away from Rook. "Or maybe one bath and then another bath."

Rook glowered. It wasn't funny. The muck-spider had been horrible, and he almost hadn't gotten away from its pincer-claws. "Leave it," he muttered, getting to his feet. Ugh. He could practically see the stench floating around him in a rancid cloud.

Ash laughed. "Or maybe ten baths. And, brothers, I know where we can steal some excellent soap."

four

Overnight, Fer had decided. "I'll come," she told Lich and Gnar in the gray hour before sunrise. But she'd only been back from visiting Grand-Jane in the human world for a night. She knew the message was urgent, but her first responsibility was always her land and its people, and she had to see to them before she left. "Tell the High Ones I'll be there as soon as I can."

The Way that was like a door into her land was only open at the turn of day into night or night into day. In a little while, dawn would arrive and Lich and Gnar would go back to the nathe. In the gray, chilly air, Gnar looked like banked embers; a dusting of ash lay over her black skin. "But you *will* come, Lady Strange, won't you?" she asked.

"I said I would," Fer answered.

"The spark here is worried," Lich said.

"I *am* worried," Gnar agreed. "Nothing has happened yet, but because of the changes you've brought here, it feels like something is about to happen. Those Lords and Ladies—the ones who came with Arenthiel and us on the hunt, when we—you know . . ."

"When you attacked my land and its people, you mean," Fer finished.

Gnar's eyes sparked. "Yes, that's what I mean."

"We're very sorry about it," Lich put in soberly.

"We are," Gnar said, then went on impatiently. "The thing is, O Strange One, the Lords and Ladies who came on the hunt—the ones who swore an oath to you that they would take off the glamories, remember?"

Fer nodded. Of course she remembered. Gnar and Lich had taken off their glamories and the land had opened and swallowed them up, and the other Lords and Ladies had sworn a binding oath to take their glamories off too, and then they had slunk back to the nathe.

"Well," Gnar said, "Lich and I were able to remove our glamories because we hadn't been wearing them for very long. The rest of the Lords and Ladies didn't take off their glamories."

"A few of them tried," Lich put in, "but they couldn't abide the change. They soon put their glamories back on again."

"They swore oaths to you, Lady, and now that the

oaths have been broken, they are forsworn," Gnar said.

Fer's stomach clenched. It was exactly as she'd feared. She knew very well that a broken oath was a really serious thing in this world, and would have serious consequences.

"The forsworn Lords and Ladies are a danger to everyone," Gnar finished. "We can't ignore them until it's too late."

"I know." Fer nodded. At least Gnar had said *we* instead of assuming the problem was Fer's alone. "I really will come as soon as I can. Okay?"

Gnar nodded, and the coals at the ends of her braids flared.

At that moment, the sun lifted into the sky and the Way opened.

"See you tomorrow!" Fer called as Gnar and Lich stepped through.

Or the next day. First she had to be absolutely sure the stain of the broken oaths hadn't touched her land. Then she'd talk to the High Ones. They were wise; they might have some advice for how to deal with what Grand-Jane had called *consequences*.

Rook wasn't sure whether Fer would be glad to see him or not. All summer long, he'd been avoiding her. When she'd gone to the nathe for that stupid contest, he'd gone with her, and he would have betrayed her then, given the chance. After that, she'd saved his life—again—but she probably wasn't very happy with him.

Still, he *hadn't* betrayed her after all, had he? And he was tied to her with that strange thread. He could feel it, warm and alive, thrumming in his chest. It meant they were friends, didn't it? Sort of? And that meant she'd help him, if he asked.

He'd tried explaining the thread to his brothers, but they wouldn't listen.

"A puck can't be tied to a Lady like that," Rip had said.

"Are you saying I'm not a puck?" Rook shot back.

"I'm not, no," Rip growled. "Just break it. It's a binding. You're better off getting rid of it."

"No," Rook had said, stubborn. He'd broken the thread twice before, once when Fer had trusted him by helping him get into the nathe, and the second time when he'd been about to betray her. If he broke the thread a third time, his friendship with Fer would be gone forever. He was surprised at how fiercely he'd fight to keep that from happening.

"She's still a Lady," Asher had put in. "We don't accept rule from anyone, not even her."

"This thread doesn't have anything to do with rule," Rook argued. "And I'm not doing it your way this time."

"Look, Pup," his brother Ash had said. "You can do it any way you like. Just use your Lady to do the test on a glamorie, all right?"

All right. He was the one with the shadow-web stuck to his hand, so he was the one who needed to find a Lord or Lady to see if what his brothers had planned would work. And Fer was a Lady, so she had to be the one to help him do that.

Before going through the Way to Fer's land, he shifted into his dog shape. Teeth were a good defense in case he ran into any of Fer's idiot wolf-guards.

Night blurred into day, and the Way opened. As he stepped through, somebody passed him going the other direction. Two somebodies. He felt a wash of flames and then a damp breath, and whoever it was went past and away, and then he was through.

He padded into a clearing flushed with the early, pink light of dawn. Fer stood in the middle of it. He froze, eyes narrowing. She looked different than she had in the summer, when he'd last seen her. Wilder. More powerful, too, but not in the way that the glamorie-wearing Lords or Ladies were powerful. Some other way.

Before, she'd always been glad to see him. This time she frowned a little. "Hello, Rook."

Well, fine. He lowered his head and growled.

"Oh, are you supposed to be fierce?" she asked.

Yes. He showed his teeth and growled again, deeper.

She raised her eyebrows. "Rook, your tail is wagging."

It was, curse it. Stupid betrayer of a tail.

"Other than that," she went on, mock seriously, "you do look extremely dangerous."

Grrrr. He spat out his shifter-tooth and blurred into his person shape.

Fer blinked and stepped back. "Wow," she said. "You look different."

He looked down at himself. It really had taken about ten baths, but Asher had stolen some excellent soap, so he'd finally scrubbed all the slime and stench off himself. All except the shadow-web stuck to his left hand. He kept his fist clenched so Fer wouldn't see how it tracked like a bit of blackened net across his palm.

His brothers had stolen some clothes for him too, so he wore the long, embroidered coat, high-collared silk shirt, trousers, and the soft leather boots of a Lord, all in shades of cream and rich brown, and he'd combed his hair back and tied it neatly with a bit of string.

Now Fer was frowning again. "Hmm," she said slowly. "You coming here dressed like that. You're up to something, aren't you?"

His brothers thought he should lie to Fer, use her like

he had before to get what they wanted. He could see the result of that, right in front of him. She didn't trust him anymore. Still, he had to try. "You don't have your glamorie, do you?"

Fer narrowed her eyes, suspicious. "No, I don't. Why do you ask?"

Hm. That's what he'd thought. He'd have to try the other plan. "I have to get to the nathe. Will you take me there?"

She stared. Then she gave a sharp shake of her head. "You must think I'm really stupid, Rook. I am going to the nathe, but there is no way I'm taking you with me."

Curse it. He'd have to try something else. Like telling the truth. The thread in his heart thrummed, as if it liked the idea. "I am up to something, yes," he said carefully. "My brothers have a plan." They hadn't told him yet what that plan was, probably because they hadn't figured it out yet exactly, but he trusted them to get it right. "We need your help. Will you help us?"

"No," she said firmly.

He pulled his left hand out of his coat pocket, where he'd been hiding it. "Fer, look at this."

She stepped closer to see.

He opened his hand. The muck-spiderweb looked like a net of black lines smudged across his palm.

"What is it?" she asked. She bent her head, inspecting it. "Does it hurt?"

"It doesn't feel like anything," he answered. He explained about how he and his brothers had gone to see the moon-spinner spider. "That's where glamories come from."

"Ohhh," she breathed, looking up. "Spun out of moonlight. That makes sense."

"This," he said, holding up his hand, "is from another spider, one that spins its web out of shadows." After they'd left the chasm, he and his brothers had crossed the rock plain again, to the spire where the moon-spinner spider spun its glamorie webs. *Just a test,* Asher had said, and Rook had bent to touch the glamorie with his web-stained hand. At the touch of the shadow-web, the sparkling silver net had turned black and crumbled away. The rot had spread, creeping across the glamorie and up the web that stretched from the spire to the ground. As the rot reached the moon-spinner spider, it scrabbled away, but then the rot caught it and its body turned black, like glass smudged with soot. All around it, the spider's web hung in greasy tatters being shredded by the wind.

Then the wind had gusted, and the last of the glamorie turned to oily dust and blew away over the surface of the rock.

"We need to test this on a Lord or Lady," Rook explained, closing his hand around the shadow-web again. "It'll destroy the glamorie they're wearing, we think." His brothers would hate what he was about to say, but he would say it anyway. "We want the same thing, the pucks and you. You don't like rule, or glamories, and we don't either. Maybe we can work together."

Fer straightened and paced away, looking around at the birch trees that edged the clearing, at their leaves shivering in the breeze and turning gold under the rising sun. Then she looked down, as if she could see deep into the ground under her feet.

He watched, wary. What would she decide?

She turned back and took a deep breath. "The glamories are a big problem. You're right about that. Some of the Lords and Ladies swore to take their glamories off and they didn't. They're forsworn—oath breakers. But . . ." She shook her head. "I'm not sure if destroying their glamories is the right thing to do. I don't know if that will fix the broken oaths." Her voice lowered as if she was talking to herself. "No, it probably wouldn't work."

He wasn't quite following. "What wouldn't work?"

"Using your web to force the forsworn Lords and Ladies to give up their glamories," she explained.

He didn't get it. "Why not force them?"

"Because that's not how I do things. I don't think it would count as a fulfilled oath anyway, if they were forced. I'll have to ask the High Ones about it." Then she narrowed her eyes and pointed at him, and that pointing finger reminded him suddenly of her grandmother. She wouldn't put up with any trickery, that meant. "If I let you come, will you help me?"

"If I can, I will," he answered truthfully.

She nodded slowly. "All right." She paused. "If we meet the Lords and Ladies—the forsworn ones—you'll be able to see what they really are, won't you? With your puck-vision? Like if they're stained or wildling, like the Mór was?"

He nodded.

"Good. Then you can come, and you can help with that. But we're there so I can see the High Ones, not for you to test your web. You have to promise that you won't touch any Lord or Lady with that shadow-web unless I say it's okay. Do you promise?"

"I do, Fer. I promise," he said, and the heart-thread in his chest gave a warm thrum, and he grinned, suddenly and surprisingly happy that she had decided to trust him again.

five

Leaving Rook to exchange growls and narrow-eyed glances with the wolf-guard Fray, Fer went up to her house in the Lady Tree. During the summer, her house had just been a roof with silken cloth for walls, more a tent than a house. Now that fall had come, it was time to put the real walls up, with rugs hung on the inside for warmth.

She felt the urgency of the *consequences* pulling at her. She couldn't spend the time she wanted making sure all was well in her own land; she'd have go to the nathe the next time the Way opened. She talked to a few deer-women about keeping an eye on the bark-borer beetles in the deep forest. Then she mixed up a healing tea for the badger-man's cough and sent one of her wolf-guards to bring it to him. After that, she took a long nap because she'd been up all night—coming through the Way from Grand-Jane's house, and then meeting with Gnar and Lich. When she woke up, she got ready. If Rook was going to look all fine and fancy for their trip to the nathe, then she had to dress up too.

Fer rummaged in the wooden trunk where she kept her clothes, pulling on her patch-jacket over her ragged T-shirt. Grand-Jane had stitched the jacket with powerful protective spells, and Fer kept cloth bags full of magical herbs in its pockets too. For her, it was stronger than any armor.

In the trunk she found her bag of herbs and medicines that she always carried with her now, along with a tiny stoppered jar of Grand-Jane's honey; she put all of that into her jacket pocket. Then she changed into the pair of jeans with the smallest holes in the knees, and found some socks and her sneakers and put those on too. Twig came in then with her wooden comb.

"Sit on the bed, Ladyfer," the fox-girl said. Fer obeyed. Twig lifted the snarled mass of Fer's hair and dropped it again. "It's so tangled," she said with a sigh, and raised the comb.

"Twig!" Fer sat up straighter. "Can you cut it off?" Her long hair was so much trouble: combing the snarls out, relying on Twig to keep it neatly braided. "Will you, I mean?"

"Yes," Twig said, and went to fetch a knife.

While she was gone, Fer called her bees to her. They were the Lady's bees, whose buzzing hums only she could understand. They flowed in through her house's doorway and buzzed around the room in a golden swarm. She'd only bring one of them with her to the nathe. The one bee settled on her patchwork sleeve. "The rest of you stay here, all right?" she asked. "I won't be gone long." As an answer, the bees swarmed out the door past Twig, who was coming back in.

Twig grinned and held up a knife. "Nice and sharp," she said, and started hacking away at the clumps of Fer's hair.

While Twig worked, Fer closed her eyes. She had a thread tying her to all the people in her land—a bond between them—and it told her if they were happy, or if they needed her, or if they were worried about something. Now that Rook was here, she could feel a thread tying her to him, too. It wasn't the same, though, as the connection she had to her people. It was warmer, somehow. It made her want to trust him. She was glad the thread was there, whatever it was.

"Ooh, that's a bad knot," she heard Twig murmur. She pulled at a snarl.

"Ow," Fer complained.

"Keep still, Ladyfer," Twig said. "It's your own fault."

It'd be her own fault too, if Rook had tricked her. He was a puck, after all, and she knew what that meant, despite the thread that connected them. He played by puck rules, and his promises might not be trustworthy.

Still, she needed his help with this. She would just have to be careful.

"All done," Twig said, and stepped back to survey her work.

Fer ran a hand over her head. Her short hair felt light, like chick-fluff. The back of her neck felt bare.

"We should come with you," the wolf-guard, Fray, said from the doorway.

"We should," Twig agreed.

Fer stood up, brushing the last long strands of chopped-off hair from her shoulders. "It'll be a quick trip," she said. "I won't be away for too long. I need you to stay here and make sure everything's all right while I'm gone. All right?"

Twig and Fray nodded grudging agreement and followed Fer down the ladder to the ground, where Rook was waiting.

Fray stalked past Fer and up to Rook; she grabbed the front of his coat and snarled something down at him.

Rook twisted in her grip and growled something back. Then she shoved him, and he stumbled away. "Stupid wolf," he muttered as Fer came up.

"Can you blame her for not liking you very much?" Fer asked.

He didn't answer, but Fer heard dark grumblings as he followed her to the Way. They waited in silence while the sun sank behind the trees. The sky darkened and the air grew chilly. Finally the first star appeared. Fer's bee lifted from the sleeve of her jacket and circled them once.

"You'll be on your best behavior, won't you, Rook?" Fer asked.

Looking unusually serious, he nodded. "I will, yes."

"Remember, you promised," Fer said as the Way opened.

"I won't forget." Rook reached out, and she took his hand, and they stepped through the Way together.

Rook stayed quiet as he followed Fer from the Lake of All Ways to the nathe. Fer was taking a chance on him— he was well aware of it—so he'd try not to be too tricksy.

The nathe was the center of all the lands. It wasn't a palace, exactly; it was like a huge, bark-covered tree stump, with moss creeping up its gray walls and roots that plunged deep into the ground. Inside, rooms and passages and a great hall called the nathewyr had been carved out of the wood.

No puck except for him had ever visited the nathe, and the last time he'd been here, they'd tried to kill him.

As he followed Fer up the gnarled steps that led to one of the nathe's many doors, they were met by a nathe-warden, a guard with rough, brown skin and greenish hair that reminded him of willow-wands. The warden glared at him.

Rook bared his teeth in a sharp grin, and felt for his shifter-tooth in his pocket. *Go ahead, willow-warden,* his grin said. *I'm ready for you.*

"Lady Gwynnefar," the guard said, "you are welcome to the nathe, but this puck is not."

Fer shrugged. "He stays, or I leave," she said, and swept past the warden. Rook ducked past the guard too, to catch up with her. As they stepped into a polished hallway, she glanced aside at him. "It's amazing how many people don't like you, Rook," she said.

"Well, I don't like them either," he grumbled. And he hadn't actually bitten the nathe-warden. He *was* on his best behavior, after all.

She kept walking. They were passing through a long hallway lit by glowing crystals when a short, gray-skinned stick-person with a tuft of green hair on its head popped out of another hallway. When it spoke, its voice was surprisingly deep and rough, like bark. "Lady!"

Fer stopped; Rook stepped up beside her. "What is it?" she asked.

The stick-person bobbed a bow. "My master. Arenthiel.

He wishes to see you. Come!" It pointed toward the other passageway.

"We-ell, I don't know," Fer said slowly. A lock of her short-cut hair curled over her forehead and she brushed it away. "I came here to see the High Ones."

"See them, too," the stick-person said. "See Arenthiel now. To talk."

Fer frowned, but Rook could see that she was about to agree. "Wait," he interrupted. "Arenthiel is your enemy, Fer." And the enemy of the pucks. "It could be a trap."

"Rook, we're in the nathe," Fer answered. "It's not a trap. Arenthiel was broken after he lost the contest and failed to steal my lands from me. You were asleep when it happened, but if you'd seen it, you'd know that he's not any threat to me."

"Oh sure he's not," he muttered.

"Just talk!" put in the stick-person.

"I'm going to see him," Fer said. "Do you want to come with me?"

Rook nodded. "They'll toss me out if I don't." Or worse.

They followed the stick-person through hallways that were strangely empty, as if all the people who lived there were hiding away in their rooms like frightened rab- bits in their burrows. Waiting for something to happen. They went up some winding stairs to an ornately carved and polished doorway, where the stick-person bowed them inside. The room was circular, carved from the dark wood and polished, with gleaming crystals set in niches in the walls. On a couch made of plump green pillows sat a shriveled, ancient creature with a face like an apple with a bite taken out of it and then left to rot.

"Hello, Arenthiel," Fer said.

Rook blinked and looked again. It really *was* him. Arenthiel. Fer's old enemy, the one who'd tried to steal the Summerlands from her, but failed. Instead of killing him, she'd sent him home to the nathe.

Arenthiel's withered face cracked into a toothless smile. "Hello, Lady," he said, and reached out with a wrinkled claw of a hand.

Fer took half a step toward him, then stopped. Not so quick to trust, Rook was glad to see.

The old creature's face fell, and then he trembled into a cough that made his whole body shake.

Fer crossed the room and knelt by his side. "That sounds awful," she said. "Have you been sick for a while?"

Arenthiel's only answer was another pitiful cough.

But Rook was sure he caught a glimpse of mischief in Arenthiel's eye. "Fer . . ." he started to warn.

"Shh," she interrupted. Then she spoke to the stick-person. "I'll need some hot water in a cup," she ordered.

The stick-person bowed and left the room, returning in just a moment with a mug full of steaming water. Fer took it, busying herself with a bag of herbs and a jar of honey she pulled from her patch-jacket pocket. Then she handed Arenthiel the tea she'd made, helping him curl his withered hands around the mug.

Rook stood staring down at Arenthiel. *Old Scrawny*, the pucks had named him. Arenthiel, who hated pucks and had wanted to hunt his brothers down and kill every last one of them.

The old creature took a sip of his tea and then grinned up at him. "You're still alive, are you, young Robin?" Arenthiel asked in a high-pitched, creaky voice.

Rook didn't bother answering such a stupid question. "Fer, you shouldn't be helping him," he said.

She put away the last of the herbs and got to her feet. "He seems pretty harmless to me." She looked from him to Arenthiel and back again. "Do what you came to help me with, Rook. Look at him with your puck-vision and tell me what you see."

Before when he'd looked into Arenthiel Rook had seen through the shell of beauty he wore to hide his rotten core. It hadn't been a glamorie that he'd worn that had made him beautiful; it'd been because he was kin to the High Ones, or so he claimed. Now, on the outside, Aren was a wrinkled husk; Rook expected to see rot on the inside, but it wasn't there. Old Scrawny was withered all the way through, but with no taint of evil.

"Well?" Fer prompted.

"He looks all right." Rook shook his head. "But he's probably up to something. He's a troublemaker."

"Takes one to know one," Arenthiel put in with a cackle.

Grrrr. Rook took a threatening step closer.

"Rook." Fer shook her head, then turned to Arenthiel. "Your servant said you wanted to talk. The tea has valerian in it and it'll make you sleepy, so you'd better make it fast."

The ancient creature was already blinking. "Wait," he muttered, and reached out with his withered stick of a hand. "Lady. Wait."

Fer crouched beside him again; Rook edged closer to listen.

"Must tell you," Arenthiel said in his cracked voice. "I am here in the nathe, at the center of all things, but I cannot leave these rooms. Cannot do anything. The High Ones' power is waning; they keep to their rooms too. Those who broke their oaths. The Forsworn." He paused to give a dry cough. "Their power grows. You must be careful. Be careful, Lady. They are here in the nathe."

"They're *here*?" Fer gasped.

"Be careful of them," Arenthiel muttered, his eyes dropping closed. "Be careful of you."

"Don't worry," Fer said, and took the mug from his hands, setting it on the floor. Getting to her feet, she gently eased Arenthiel back against the pillows. The old creature sighed, and slept.

six

Arenthiel was right. She needed to be careful. As Fer led Rook through the winding passageways of the nathe, she remembered something the Mór had told her. The Mór, who had been forsworn herself. *Our oaths bind us together,* the crow-woman had said. *When an oath is broken there is a price. And it is always more than the oath breaker can pay.*

What price were the forsworn Lords and Ladies paying? Fer wondered. Their broken oaths might mean the usual connection a Lord or Lady had with their lands and their people had been cut. Evidently they had abandoned their own lands and were taking over the nathe.

The High Ones might not be able to stop them, Fer realized. They didn't wear glamories; they had never seemed to rule by demanding obedience, or with might and muscle. Their power had come from somewhere else. From the weight of wisdom and quiet strength. But now they were hiding in their rooms as if their power was waning.

The Forsworn could be very dangerous indeed if they were drawing power from their broken oaths, here at the center of everything.

Maybe she should try to find them here at the nathe and talk to them. And then, if they wouldn't fulfill their oaths to her, would she ask Rook to touch them with his shadow-stained hand? She shook her head. No. The Forsworn had to fulfill their oaths because they knew it was right, not because somebody forced them to do it.

Outside the nathewyr, Fer found Gnar and Lich waiting for her.

"Lady Strange," Gnar said with a flickering grin. "You've cut off all your hair. And you brought that puck with you." She gave Rook a long, appreciative look. "He looks much nicer now than he did before."

Fer heard Rook give a low growl.

"Thank you for coming, Lady Gwynnefar," Lich said with a proper bow. "And I think your hair looks very nice."

It was funny how these two were always with each other. Fer gave them a little bow in return. "Are you . . ."

She wasn't sure what they called it here. Back in the human world it would be *going out* or *dating*. "Are you, um, bound to each other?"

"Ha!" Gnar said. And shot a fiery glance toward the swamp-boy.

"Fire and water do not mix, Lady," Lich said soberly.

But Fer saw the steamy look he gave Gnar in return. They weren't *together*, maybe, but they were something.

"The High Ones are waiting," Gnar said, and opened the door to the nathewyr.

To Fer's surprise, the great hall was empty and dark, except the platform at the other end, which was lit by a few dim crystals.

"We can't come in with you," Lich whispered.

With Rook a step behind her, and her bee a comforting presence on her jacket sleeve, Fer set across the echoing, empty hall. When she'd been here before, the High Ones' wisdom and power had filled the room. It was a place where time didn't pass; it just was. This had been a place of silence and stillness, of darkness and depth, and of old, old age. It had made her feel small, and very young.

But now it was a place of empty echoes.

As she approached the platform, the two High Ones gazed down at her. To her they looked the same as always—hair as bright as braided sunlight, dappled skin,

Grand County Middle School
MEDIA CENTER
Moab, Utah 84532

white robes edged with gold, ancient eyes as deep as forest pools. They were beautiful even though they didn't wear glamories, and never had.

"What do you see when you look at them, Rook?" Fer whispered.

"They are what they look like," he said, without lowering his voice at all. "They're not liars like the rest of them." The rest of the Lords and Ladies, he meant. He stopped, and Fer stopped too and turned to face him. "They look different too." He shook his head. "They're tired."

Fer turned back and studied the High Ones. Now that he pointed it out, she could see it too. Their golden beauty looked tarnished somehow. Hopefully they'd still be able—and willing—to help. They had tested her before admitting she was the true Lady of the Summerlands. She still didn't know if they approved of her or not.

Fer knew she was expected to kneel to the High Ones and speak solemnly. Instead she climbed onto the platform and gave them a quick bow. "Hi," she said. Her voice sounded muffled in the heavy air.

"Lady Gwynnefar," one of the High Ones responded. Her voice was cool and smooth, like water in a stream running over stones. "You know why we have called you here."

Fer nodded. "Some of the Lords and Ladies are for-sworn because they won't take off their glamories. I guess they're causing problems."

The High One inclined her head in a graceful nod. "The oaths they have broken were sworn to you."

"So you want me to deal with the consequences," Fer said. She understood that. She just didn't know what role the High Ones were going to play in this. "Are you going to help me?" she asked.

The High Ones gazed at her, their faces blank. "We have summoned you," one said.

"You are part human, Gwynnefar," added the other, "and you have brought change to these lands. We are unchanging."

"You act alone in this," said the first.

Fer felt a sharp pang of dismay at that. And then a tingle of warmth from the thread that connected her to Rook.

"No, she doesn't," he put in from a step behind her, his voice rough. "I'm with her."

Fer glanced over her shoulder. "Thanks, Rook," she whispered. Then she turned back to the High Ones. They were truly a mystery. They were ageless. Around them, time slowed to a standstill. Yet they seemed to want the change that she brought to the lands.

The High Ones rose from their thrones and Fer

caught another glimpse of their weariness. As they turned to leave, one of them, blank-faced as always, paused and spoke to Fer in a low voice. "Gwynnefar. We cannot see what is coming to pass. Yet we sense that danger awaits us all."

Yes, she knew that. "I have to get them to fulfill their oaths, right?" she asked. "That will mean they're not forsworn anymore, and nothing bad will happen?"

"If you can," one of the High Ones breathed.

"But I can't force them to do it," Fer said.

The High One passed a dappled hand over Fer's head, then sighed. "Do be careful, Gwynnefar. Do."

To Fer's surprise, the High One turned next to Rook, who took a wary step back as she raised her hand. "And you, young puck," she said, and Fer thought she saw the faintest smile ripple across her calm face. The High One stepped closer to him, then reached out and touched his chest, right over his heart. "Stay true."

And then they were gone.

seven

Rook followed Fer through the darkened hall toward the double doors.

The place where the High One had touched him tingled—it was right where the heart thread tied him to Fer. What had she meant, *stay true*? He was keeping his promise to Fer; he wasn't planning any betrayal. And he was doing really well so far, with the best behavior.

He shook his head. Taking a few quick steps, he caught up with Fer, then took his left hand out of his coat pocket and opened it, reminding Fer about the shadow-web, the smudged black lines that crossed his palm. "It's time for the test?"

Fer stopped and faced him. "I have to find the Forsworn, but I only want to talk to them. We're not using the web." She pointed to his hand.

Rook frowned. The Forsworn were dangerous. The Mór had been like that. She had broken her oath to her Lady, Fer's mother, and then everything in that land had gone wrong—the winter had frozen out the spring; the people had turned wildling; the wild hunt had spilled blood, staining the land even more.

"How many Forsworn are there, do you know?" he asked.

"Around ten, I think," Fer answered. "Before I try anything else, I have to talk to them, convince them to take the glamories off."

"Fer, they're not going to—" he started.

With an echoing boom, the double doors of the nathewyr swung open. Four Ladies and a Lord loomed in the doorway, shadows robed in gray, dark against the brighter light outside.

Rook felt a prickle at the back of his neck. His dog self would be growling and sniffing the air for danger. Fer didn't want him using the shadow-web, so with his right hand, he felt in his pocket for his shifter-tooth. If there were a fight, his dog form would be best.

Fer's bee felt the same threat; it lifted from Fer's sleeve to buzz around her head in tight circles.

The five robed shapes stepped farther into the hall. As one, they lifted their hands and jerked back their hoods.

The Forsworn. They dazzled; the nathewyr was lit brightly by the brilliance of their glamories. Beside him, Fer gasped and ducked her head, blinded.

Rook blinked and used his puck-vision to peer beyond the brilliant light. He gave a grim nod. It was the Forsworn, their true selves shriveled and ugly behind their overbright glamories.

Beside him, Fer stumbled; then she straightened, as if throwing off the effect of all those glamories lined up against her. She was a Lady. She couldn't see through the glamories, but they couldn't affect her much either. They couldn't rule her.

"She's here," said one of the Ladies to the other Forsworn, and stepped forward. She appeared to be a tall, slender birch woman with pale skin splashed here and there with black, and hair like golden leaves woven together. Behind her glamorie, Rook could see, she was something ancient and dark, like a spindly trunk with branches bare of leaves. She looked down her long nose at Fer, then cast a sneer of deep disgust at him. He knew that one—the *nasty puck* look.

The other four Forsworn spread out slowly, forming a circle with Fer and Rook in the middle.

Rook felt a growl building in his chest. He gripped his shifter-tooth and pulled his web-smudged hand out of his pocket, ready to use it if he had to.

The Forsworn glided over the stone floor, closing in around Fer and Rook.

"Wait," Fer said clearly.

To Rook's surprise, the Forsworn stopped.

"I just want to talk to you for a second," Fer said. "You swore oaths to take off your glamories. You swore them to me. Now you're forsworn, and I have to put things right. Will you give up your glamories willingly?"

"You are human," the Birch-Lady said, "and thus you are nothing more than an insect caught in a river of time rushing past. You change, and you cannot understand us. We will never remove our glamories." The other Forsworn nodded, agreeing with this.

"I am a Lady, just like you," Fer said steadily. "I am connected to the Summerlands and its people, just as you are connected to your own lands and people."

"You think you are like us?" the Forsworn Lord asked from behind them. Glancing over his shoulder, Rook saw that he had shiny, kelplike hair and skin tinted green, and his glamorie shone like the sun glinting off the sea. Under the glamorie, Rook saw, the Sea-Lord looked like a crab-man crouching in a watery cave, his beady eyes watching, his claws ready to reach out and *snap*. "You are nothing like us, human girl." He looked around at the Ladies, and they nodded, and he continued. "If we take off the glamories, time will flow and we will be swept away.

Why not have time circle around us like a whirlpool? Why not remain unchanging, as we are?"

Fer's eyes widened as if she'd suddenly realized something. "If you don't change, then you're not really alive. Everything changes all the time; it has to." She'd gone very pale. "If you won't change, then your lands won't either. That will be the price you pay for breaking your oaths. Your lands and your people will suffer. You're connected to them. Don't you feel any love for them at all?"

The Birch-Lady spoke. Her voice was beautiful, like a breeze rustling through leaves. But her words were cold. "That does not matter anymore. We will never remove our glamories." She nodded sharply at the other Forsworn. "Now. Get rid of the puck and take her."

At her order, the Sea-Lord and two Ladies lunged forward, grabbing Fer, who shouted and struggled in their grip.

In a flash, Rook shifted into his dog shape; snarling, he leaped at one of the Ladies, slashing with his teeth. She shrieked and fell back, and drops of blood spattered from her arm. Rook whirled to snap at the Lord. He and the other Lady let Fer go and backed away.

"Rook, we have to get out of here," Fer gasped.

He shifted back to his person form. "We do, yes," he said grimly.

The Birch-Lady strode forward. Behind her, the other Forsworn closed in.

Rook growled and raised his web-stained hand.

"Rook, *no*—" Fer started.

"Take her!" the Birch-Lady cried, and reached out to seize Fer.

Instead Rook stepped between them and grabbed the Forsworn Lady's arm with his web-stained hand.

"Ugh!" she cried, and jerked away.

For a moment, he thought it hadn't worked. Then she lifted her arm and stared at it. "What did you do, Puck?" She turned a venomous look onto Fer. "What has your puck done to me?"

As they watched, the glamorie covering the Lady's arm burned away, turning to greasy black dust that sifted to the floor.

"What have you *done*?" she screamed. The rot had set into her glamorie. It spread up her arm and over her shoulder, and she scrabbled at it with her other hand, trying to hold it back. The rot crept on, and she clawed at it as her glamorie shredded into muck and ruin.

The Sea-Lord and other Ladies scrambled away from her, their eyes wide.

The rot crept like a blackened crust up her neck and over her face, and the last of the glamorie melted away, and her screams turned to moans as the hidden creature was revealed. She stood for a moment, hunched and gnarled, then collapsed to the floor, covered with the muck of the rotten glamorie.

The thing that had been the Birch-Lady dragged herself over the stone floor, reaching with one spindly, muck-smeared arm toward the Lord and other Ladies, who backed away, horrified. "Give me . . . glamorie," she moaned. "Just for . . . little while. I will give it back, I swear."

"Don't let it touch you," one of the Ladies screeched.

A howl rose up from the thing on the floor. The stench of the shadow-spinner spider filled the hall. The howl turned into a moaning sigh, and the creature subsided onto the floor like a heap of sticks, and lay still.

The Sea-Lord edged forward, then bent to examine the Birch-Lady. "I think it's dead." He and the Ladies backed away until they stood in the double doorway of the nathewyr, as if being too near the dead Lady would contaminate them.

One of the Ladies pointed at Fer with a trembling finger. "*You* did this. Your coming brings terrible changes upon us. Abomination!"

"Let us flee," said the Sea-Lord. "Quickly. Before the human and her puck kill us all."

The Lord and Ladies scurried out the door, leaving Rook and Fer standing in the nathewyr with the dead

Birch-Lady in a heap on the floor.

Rook clenched his hand around the shadow-web. He hadn't told Fer about what had happened after he and his brothers had tested the web. The glamorie web had turned to dust, yes. But as he and his brothers had left the bare rock land of the spiders, the ruined moon-spinner spider had scuttled to the top of the spire, where it had clung, keening a high-pitched wail and reaching with its long legs toward the moon, lost to it forever. Its cry had been full of horror and desolation.

And, he realized now, full of death.

eight

Her heart pounding, Fer looked away from the heap of muck-covered sticks that had been the Birch-Lady.

A Lady, dead. *Dead.*

How had she let this happen?

A few paces away, Rook stood with his hand clenched around the bit of shadow-web on his palm, staring at the dead Lady.

Rook.

Had he . . . ? He *had*. He had broken his promise. And look what had happened. She shivered with the horror of it.

That's where she had gone wrong. Trusting Rook. When she spoke, her voice sounded strangely calm. "You promised not to use the shadow-web."

"What?" He blinked and looked up at her. "Fer, I did it to protect you."

"You shouldn't have. You promised you wouldn't use the web, but you did. All along, you wanted to do your test, didn't you?"

Rook had gone very pale. "The moon-spinner spider," he said, and she realized that he was shaking, too. "After its web was destroyed it—" He shook his head. "I'm not sure. It was gone. It might've died."

She felt a sudden flare of anger. "The spider *died*? And you didn't think to tell me this? Look!" she said, pointing at the thing on the floor. "Look at what we've done! It's awful." The horror of it all washed over her. She should have known this would happen. "I should never have trusted you." Her bee circled her head, buzzing anxiously. "You only came here to make trouble, not to help me. Your brothers have some plan, and they sent you to trick me. Again! Admit it!"

"N-no—" he stuttered. "Fer, I'll never use this again." He held up his web-smudged hand. "I promise."

"Oh, sure." She jerked away from him. "Your promises are worth nothing, Rook. You're a *puck*," she said, saying the word as if it were a curse. "You think you're outside friendship with anybody but your brothers." A little part of her brain knew she was being unreasonable, that Rook had been trying to help, that she was in shock from the horrible death of the Birch-Lady. Another part of her was revolted by what he'd done—what they'd *both* done. She closed her eyes and pushed him with her mind—*away*.

"Fer, no!" she heard Rook say, his voice desperate. "Don't break it."

But it was too late. She pushed, and she felt something snap.

As the broken end of that something crashed into her, she felt it like a punch to the chest. It brought with it a sudden sadness that almost swamped her.

She opened her eyes to see Rook flinching away, as if he'd been struck. "Oh, curse it, Fer," he said brokenly. "That was the third time."

The third time . . .

He was talking about the thread of their friendship. It was gone. They weren't connected anymore. She blinked her eyes fast to keep the tears from welling up. Then her heart, free of its thread, hardened. "I shouldn't have brought you with me. If you hadn't been here, this wouldn't have happened."

In response, Rook's eyes flamed. His voice turned bitter. "Oh, sure. It's easy to blame the puck, isn't it, Lady Gwynnefar?"

"That's enough, Rook," she said, swallowing down her sadness and her anger. "I'm going home to the

Summerlands. We're not friends anymore. I don't want to see you ever again."

Fer fled.

She didn't want to tell the High Ones what had just happened or figure out how she was going to deal with the rest of the Forsworn now that one of them was dead.

She just wanted to be *home*, in the Summerlands, where she belonged. She needed to be there, to protect her land from whatever taint arose from the Forsworn ones' broken oaths.

Keeping her head lowered, she hurried through the nathe. Leaving behind the best friend she'd ever had, even though he'd never really been her friend at all.

Her bee buzzed worriedly around her as she headed outside and down one of the gnarled stairways leading from the nathe. She wished Phouka had come with her so she could ride quickly away; instead she started running across the wide lawn that lay before the nathe, and then through the forest to the outer wall. Beyond that was the Lake of All Ways.

The sky overhead was gray and glassy, the same color as the Lake, which shimmered like a mirror in the silvery light. The air was cold and still. She paused to catch her breath and hunched into her patchwork jacket. She shivered, but it wasn't from the cold. Then she went on to the Lake, her feet crunching over the pebbles that lined the shore.

All the Ways to all the lands opened here. It was nearly sunrise in her world, and the Way leading there would be open in a moment. Then she would be home.

She crouched at the edge of the water. As a Lady, she had the power to open any Way from here. Even the Way that led back to the human world. She could be with her grandma in half an hour, the time it took to step through the Way and then run down the gravel roads to her house. It was easy to imagine what Grand-Jane would say if Fer told her what had happened. Fer could *see* her, tall, gray-haired, wearing a knitted cardigan and a stern look.

You made a mistake, my girl, Grand-Jane would say. *Now what are you going to do to fix it?*

Then her grandma would open her arms, and Fer would run to her for a hug and a cup of tea and a long talk about how she would set things right.

No. She had to deal with this alone. A sob surged up in her chest, but she gulped it down.

She reached out for the Way. The power tingled in her fingers, and she touched the surface of the water. The Way to her land opened.

She stood and lifted her foot to step into it—and then she felt a rush of wind that shoved her backward. A figure robed in gray stepped out of the Lake. It grabbed her arm, and she was jerked from the Way. Her feet stumbled on the pebbly shore. She caught a glimpse of brilliant light quickly hidden; then several tall figures hooded in gray surrounded her.

The Forsworn! One of them pinned her arms behind her. She kicked and struggled, but the hands holding her were like iron.

"Let go!" she shouted.

"You've left us no choice," one of them hissed.

"Help!" she got out, and then a cloth came down over her head—a bag. She felt the tingle of a Way opening—not the Way into her own land; somewhere else—and felt herself being dragged into it.

No!

She struggled harder, and wrenched an arm free. Her power to open Ways surged up in her hand and she felt the Way to the Summerlands start to open.

"Put her out," she heard a cold voice say.

Fer felt a sharp pain in her head, and everything went dark.

nine

Rook's heart hurt where the thread had broken. It felt like shards of glass were jabbing him in the chest. Twice before he'd snapped the thread that connected him to Fer, and it hadn't been this bad. But breaking something for a third time—that made it matter. That made it something that could never be fixed.

He took a deep, shaky breath. Then another.

All right. The first thing he had to do was get out of the nathe without some stupid nathe-warden catching him and tossing him into an underground prison cell.

And then . . .

And then he'd figure out the next thing.

He cast one more glance at the dead Birch-Lady. Then he looked again. Had she moved? He stepped closer, then crouched beside her. The only light came from the doorway. In the dimness, the Birch-Lady was a person-shaped bundle of sticks and dried leaves, all covered with the stinking muck of the rotten glamorie, her face so withered he could barely make out her eyes. But . . .

Those eyes blinked and looked back at him.

"You're not dead," he said aloud. He glanced at the doorway. But no, it was too late to go after Fer to tell her. Too late for anything with Fer.

The Birch-Lady sighed and shifted with a rustling of twigs.

He couldn't abandon her; he had to find some help. Getting to his feet, he went to the doorway and peered out. The carved hallway was empty and dim, lit only by one crystal in a niche in the wall.

Hmm. The trick would be finding somebody to help the Birch-Lady without getting caught himself. He could get to Old Scrawny's rooms from here; he'd tell the old villain and then get out. He flicked his shifter-tooth into his mouth and, in his dog shape, slunk like a shadow along the edge of the hallway and up a winding set of stairs.

He paused to sniff the air, to smell the way to Old Scrawny's rooms.

Then he smelled something else—willow branches and bow and arrow and sharp knives. Nathe-warden.

"There's the puck!" came a shout.

Without even a glance over his shoulder, he leaped into a run, bounding down a corridor, his paws skidding on the smooth floor as he rounded a corner.

"This way!" came another shout.

Curse it. He'd spent time in one of the nathe's prison cells deep underground, and it wasn't someplace he wanted to visit again.

He skidded to a stop at a place where five passageways met, not sure which way to go. Then, down one long hallway, one of the short stick-people that acted as servants in the nathe leaned out of a shadow and beckoned to him.

From behind him came more shouts and the *pad-pad-pad* of quick feet running over polished wood.

They'd have him in a moment.

Hsst!

His ears flicked toward the sound. The stick-person waved wildly and hissed again.

Nothing else for it. Quickly he dashed down the hallway. With surprising speed, the stick-person led him on, its green-tufted head bobbing along before him. It swerved and he scrambled to keep up, heading along another hallway and then up a winding stair to an ornately carved door that he recognized.

Arenthiel's room.

From the stairs came the sound of feet coming up.

Rook spit out the shifter-tooth and stowed it in the pocket of his long, embroidered coat. Then he threw open the door, reached back and dragged the stick-person inside, and snapped the door closed behind them. He froze, listening. The wardens' footsteps paused outside the door. He held his breath.

"He's not up here," he heard after a long moment, and the footsteps went down the stairs again.

He leaned against the door and breathed a sigh of relief. Then he looked around the room. It was the same as before: dark, polished walls, crystals for light, and Arenthiel—Old Scrawny—huddled on a couch made of plump, green cushions.

"Young puck!" Arenthiel said with a cackle. "In trouble again, are you?"

A stupid question, not worth answering.

"I told my servants to keep an eye out for you and Gwynnefar once you were done talking to the High Ones. Where is she?"

Rook shook his head.

"Not here? Well, you come here. Sit down." Arenthiel patted the cushion beside him with a gnarled hand. "I want to talk to you."

"Well, I don't want to talk to you," Rook muttered. He didn't want to sit next to Old Scrawny either, so he sat on the floor by the door instead. He waited a stubborn moment, and then added, "One of the Forsworn is . . ." Not injured, exactly, or sick. "She's lost her glamorie," he continued. "She needs help."

Old Scrawny straightened. "Where?" he asked briskly.

"Nathewyr," Rook answered.

Arenthiel nodded and summoned his stick-people servants, who scurried off to find the Birch-Lady.

Rook gave a ragged sigh and put his head down on his knees. What a mess this all was.

He was a puck, which meant he shouldn't mind mess, but this was different.

"What's the matter?" Arenthiel asked in his high, creaky voice.

Rook gave him a baleful look. "It's not your business." He was only hiding here until the nathe-wardens got tired of searching for him. He put his head down again.

"It is too my business," the old creature huffed, and went on as if talking to himself. "It's my business more than anybody's." Then, louder, he said, "You've had a falling-out with your friend; that's clear. Now, come over here where I can get a good look at you."

Rook ignored him.

Arenthiel coughed, a dry and crackling sound. "I need more of that tea she brought me," he complained.

And then, after a pause, "She's a kind girl, isn't she, your Gwynnefar? But she has fierceness in her too, I would say."

Ignoring him was not working very well.

He heard the old creature sigh. "She wore the glamorie twice, but only for a short time, and she doesn't understand it."

Rook looked up.

"I've never worn one, so I don't truly understand it either," Arenthiel went on. "But I do know that the Forsworn and their glamories pose a terrible threat to all the lands." He raised a withered finger and pointed at Rook.

"Don't point at me like that, Old Scrawny," he interrupted. He hated when people did that. It never led to anything good.

"Ha!" Arenthiel cackled. "I like my puck name, you know. It's so descriptive!" He jabbed with his pointing finger, suddenly fierce. "You have to help her."

Fer, he meant. Rook shook his head. "She doesn't want my help."

"She needs her friends now, more than she ever has before," Arenthiel said. "Don't you think, Robin?" he added, using Rook's false name, the name pucks gave to people they distrusted, which meant everyone, just about.

Rook didn't have any answer to that. "I told you, it's

not your business," he growled.

"She was always a friend to you, wasn't she?" Arenthiel asked slyly.

Rook remained stubbornly silent for a long moment. Finally he nodded. "She was, yes." Fer had become friends with him when he'd been thrice-sworn to the Mór and bound by her to keep Fer from finding her place in the land. Fer had insisted she was his friend even when he'd been sent by his brother-pucks to betray her. She had trusted him, even when she shouldn't have. She had saved his life how many times now? He thought back, counting it up.

Five times.

And what had he done in return? He'd broken his promise to her, and he'd broken her thread of friendship twice, hardly even thinking about what he was doing.

"Stay true to her, Puck," Arenthiel said solemnly.

Rook stared at him, startled. *Stay true*. That's what the High One had said to him.

It was a stupid thing to say to a puck, really. All the people of all the lands thought pucks were betrayers. Oath breakers. Outcast for a reason. True to nothing and no one. But they were wrong. *Nobody* was more true than a puck.

His bond with his brothers was stronger than anything. Stronger than any pale oaths or promises. Pucks never bonded that way with anyone else but another puck.

"She needs you," Arenthiel prodded.

If he really did *stay true* to Fer, it would be a bond like the one he shared with his brothers. Could he do it?

"Well?" Arenthiel asked.

He could, yes. "All right," Rook growled before Arenthiel could point that wizened finger at him again. He would show Fer what it really meant to be friends with a puck. He would stay true.

The Forsworn, Arenthiel said, were very dangerous. "Far worse than the Mór was," he added. "We'll have to figure out some way to stop them."

"We?" Rook asked. "You hate pucks. You tried to hunt down and kill my brothers. I'm not helping you."

Arenthiel gave a dry cough that almost sounded like a laugh. "Oh, no. I would never suggest such a thing."

"You just did suggest it," Rook grumbled.

"A slip of the tongue," Arenthiel said. "Never mind it. Now, where was I?" He tapped his chin and pursed his lips. "Ah! The Forsworn. The fact that they *are* forsworn must be affecting their lands, just as it did for the Mór after she killed her Lady. We must find out how, exactly, and we must find out what they intend to do."

"There's that *we* again," Rook muttered. One of the

stick-people came up to him then and gave him a slab of bread and cheese. He'd rather have a nice, plump rabbit, but bread and cheese would do. He took a big bite.

"The question is," Arenthiel went on musingly, "what is to be done about their glamories?"

Then the bite turned to ashes in his mouth. He gulped it down. "The Birch-Lady. I'm the one who did that to her," he said.

He set down his food then and crossed the room to show Arenthiel his web-stained hand. He started to explain about where the glamorie came from, and the shadow-spinner spider.

"Yes, yes," Arenthiel interrupted impatiently. "I know more about the spiders than you do."

Rook narrowed his eyes, suspicious. "You do? Why?"

"Can I tell you a story?" Arenthiel asked.

A *story*? "No, you can't tell me any stupid story," Rook answered.

"Too bad. I am." Arenthiel settled in. "The Lords and Ladies didn't always wear the glamories, Puck. They were once like your Lady, Gwynnefar. True to their people and their lands. But!" He raised a bony finger. "One of the High Ones corrupted them. He was beautiful and he wanted glittering, unchanging people around him always, and he found the spider to spin a still, chill beauty out of moonlight. He gave the glamories to the people and made them Lords and Ladies. He thought he was making them powerful, but he was wrong. He was making them slaves."

"You did this?" Rook asked, startled. "You were one of the High Ones?"

"Well, I still am, in a way," Arenthiel said with a dry cough. "It's just not as obvious as it was before."

"Because you're a troublemaker," Rook added. Arenthiel was right—it took one to know one.

Arenthiel's answer was a snort of laughter. "That's right. Now, go on. You can see why this interests me. Tell me how you took the glamorie from the Forsworn."

"I didn't think it would hurt her," Rook tried to explain. He told Aren about the horrible moment when he'd touched the Birch Lady and she'd shriveled up and howled when her glamorie had been stripped away.

"Oh, dear. That is very bad, Robin. You weren't careful," Aren said. "Neither was Gwynnefar. It was a stupid mistake the two of you made, forcing a change like that."

"It was, yes," Rook found himself agreeing. Really, they were lucky the Birch-Lady hadn't died of it. Maybe she still would. "I promised Fer I wouldn't use this again." He raised his web-stained hand.

"Hmmmm. See that you keep that promise." The

ancient creature sighed and was silent for a while, sitting with his eyes closed.

Maybe he'd fallen asleep. Rook went back to his bread and cheese.

"Well, then," Arenthiel said suddenly. "When you go to the Summerlands, you'll have to—"

"No," Rook interrupted. "I told you. Fer doesn't want to see me. I'm not going there." At least, not yet. "I have to do something first to show her she can trust me."

"Trust, is it?" Arenthiel said with a toothless grin. "Well, then." He was silent for a few moments. Then he yawned. "It's time for my nap."

"Then go to sleep," Rook said grumpily.

"In a moment." The bony finger came up again, pointed. "But first tell me what you're going to do, Puck."

That was the question. He thought back to what had happened. "One of the Forsworn is the Sea-Lord. I've been to his lands before. I can go there again and see how his broken oath is affecting his lands."

Old Arenthiel nodded. "It could be nothing. Or it could be very bad. You must find out, then come back and tell me."

Rook gave a shrug as his answer. He wasn't taking orders from Old Scrawny, whether he was really a High One or not.

Aren frowned, suddenly serious. "We must be careful,

Robin." He waved a wrinkled claw of a hand. "Yes, yes, I know there is no *we* for you and me. That's fine. But listen to me now. Somehow the Forsworn must be persuaded to remove their glamories and fulfill their oaths. Until they do, they are very dangerous. Not necessarily in what they do. They are oath breakers, and that means that they are dangerous in what they *are*."

ten

Fer was asleep in the Lady Tree, which swayed in the wind like a ship at sea.

With a start, she opened her eyes, and a room swooped around her; dizzy, she closed her eyes again. Oh, such a pain in her head, and the floor was awfully cold and hard. "Twig?" she croaked. "Fray?"

Then she remembered the figures in gray—the Forsworn—who had grabbed her at the Lake of All Ways. Her eyes popped open.

Fer was *not* in the Lady Tree. Holding her head, she sat up. Her stomach lurched at the movement. With her fingers she felt the back of her skull. A tender lump, but no blood. Too bad about cutting off all of her hair; if she'd had her braid, she might not have gotten such a bump.

She looked down at herself. She still had her patchwork jacket on, at least. That was something.

She surveyed the room she was in. It was circular, about ten paces across. The floor was made of close-fitted stones. The walls were of the same gray stone with thick layers of mortar in the cracks between each one. Carefully Fer climbed to her feet, looking up. The walls stretched up to a flat ceiling—more stone—way over-head. In the ceiling was an open trapdoor that showed a flat, gray sky.

She was in a tower.

She turned in a circle. The tower only had walls; there was no door, no windows.

The Forsworn ones who'd grabbed her at the Lake of All Ways had put her here, no doubt. It was a prison. They must have lowered her down here from the opening in the ceiling, high above. "Ooookay." She took a shaky breath. Then another. The air felt strange. Heavy, as if it was weighing her down. And it was cold with the chill of underground caves.

Fer shivered and her head ached, and she sat down with her back against the curving wall. A muffled buzzing sound came from one of her jacket pockets. She opened it up, and her bee bumbled out. It wavered around her head once, then dropped onto her sleeve. She cupped her hand around it, and it buzzed against her palm. It meant she wasn't completely alone, anyway.

She rubbed her sore head and looked up at the trapdoor. At some point the Forsworn would have to come back, if only to lower her some food and water. Maybe they'd have a bucket on a rope. That would be her chance to escape. Dizzy, she rested her head against her knees and tried to think.

The Forsworn hated change. She was human, and she had the power to change things. The Forsworn had put her here, she guessed, because she was a danger to them.

They were right about that. Her thoughts bumped up against the memory of the Birch-Lady's death. But she didn't want to think about that. It led her to Rook and his latest betrayal, and she *really* didn't want to think about that. Her chest still ached where she'd broken their shared thread of friendship.

After a long time, she opened her eyes. Overhead, the square of sky framed by the trapdoor had turned dark gray. Evening was coming on. She got to her feet and, keeping one hand on the wall to steady herself, made a circuit of the room. Surely her captors would come soon, to bring her some dinner.

Strange, though. She'd been here for hours, and she didn't feel the least bit hungry. Or thirsty. Or tired.

Maybe it was because the air here was so heavy. It

made her feel slow. She went around the edge of the room again. The air was as thick as honey; she practically had to trudge through it. She couldn't hear anything from outside the tower either; the silence pressed against her ears.

As the night came on, the tower-room darkened. Fer settled down against the wall again, pulling the patch-jacket tightly around her for warmth. Her bee crawled up to her collar and nestled against her neck; it felt soft and comforting.

Sleep didn't come. She stared out at nothing. After a while, Fer got up again and, in the darkness, circled the room once more. The stone walls felt rough and slightly damp under her fingers; in the dark, she traced the mortared cracks between each block of stone. Around and around she walked.

Fer hardly noticed the morning coming on, and then she realized that the stone walls had emerged from the darkness, gray and grim. She looked down at her patch-work jacket just to see a splash of color. Even the jacket looked washed-out in the dull light.

Morning. The Forsworn would have to come soon.

It was strange, though. She'd been awake all night, walking around the room, and she wasn't a bit tired. She wasn't hungry, either, or thirsty.

She stopped and stared up at the open trapdoor in

the ceiling. A few dust motes hung in the morning light that shone in. Dust should float in the air, glinting in the light. These dust motes just hung there. Not moving.

"Oh, no," she said, and the heavy silence swallowed up her words.

Some kind of spell was on the tower. Time didn't pass inside these walls; it stood still. Frozen. That meant . . .

She clenched her fists, suddenly frightened. This was the power of the Forsworn, unchanging and uncaring. If time didn't pass inside the tower, it meant she was stuck in it, like a bee stuck in a jar of honey. She wouldn't get hungry or thirsty or tired, and no matter how long she was here she would never get any older. She would be like them—never changing.

Her breath came fast. What was she going to *do*?

Fer felt a flood of despair wash through her. She had really, *really* messed things up.

And then she had blamed Rook for it. She closed her eyes, remembering his stricken face after she'd broken the thread of their friendship.

But no. Rook had promised to tell her exactly what he was up to, and he hadn't. He was a troublemaker, and it *was* his fault, at least partly. And the thing he'd said after she'd broken their heart-thread.

Curse it, Fer, he'd said. *That was the third time.*

The third time the thread had been broken, he meant, and the pain of it really did have the power of three behind it. He must have broken the thread twice before, then. She wanted to forgive him for that, as she'd forgiven other things he'd done. She wanted to say, *Oh, he's a puck, he plays by different rules.* But she couldn't do it this time. Her heart hardened. He had never truly been her friend.

She sat with her back to the cold stone wall and felt more alone than she'd ever felt in her entire life. Tears streamed down her face, and she put her head down on her knees and cried for a long time. Maybe she did deserve to be here. A Lady was dead, killed because of Rook's broken promise, but also because of her own carelessness. She was away from her land, which needed her just as much as she needed to be there. Her people would think she'd abandoned them. She was far from Grand-Jane, when she'd promised to visit more often. Weeks would be slipping past in the human world while she was stuck here in this timeless place. Weeks, or months. Or even more.

After a while, she lifted her head. Sniffling, she wiped her eyes. All right. Crying wasn't getting her anywhere.

She really was going to be alone here forever unless she did something about it. The Summerlands people thought she was at the nathe. The High Ones and Gnar and Lich wouldn't know to look for her; once they found out about the death of the Birch-Lady, they'd think she'd run away. And Rook—he'd probably gone back to his brothers, and he certainly wouldn't notice that she was missing.

While she'd been thinking and crying and not doing anything, more time had passed outside. The sky over the trapdoor had darkened and lightened a few times; she'd lost track of how many. Days, maybe. She had all the time in the world, but no time left to waste.

"Fer," she said aloud just to hear the sound of a voice. "Remember what Grand-Jane said. Don't forget that you're *human*." She had her own human power, the power to change, to grow, to *live*. Maybe it would be enough to break the spell the Forsworn had put on this tower.

She got to her feet. "Bee," she said, and the bee buzzed from her sleeve to land on the finger she held up. Sending it away would leave her more alone, and there wasn't much chance of it helping, but she had to try. "Go and find my true friends," she told it. Fray and Twig, she meant, in the Summerlands. "If you can, lead them back here." She raised her hand, and the bee lifted from her finger. "All right?"

Zmmmmrmmrmmm, the bee answered—*yes.* It climbed

through the heavy air to the trapdoor. Then it was a dark spot against the sky, and then, with a buzz, it was gone.

Fer took a deep breath. Now she had to figure out a way to break the power of the Forsworn and escape.

eleven

Rook waited in Old Scrawny's rooms until night. The stick-servants had brought the wizened Birch-Lady back with them, and they'd cleaned the glamorie-muck off her and put her to bed. Arenthiel said he didn't know if she'd recover or not, that they'd have to wait and see. For now, all she was doing was weeping and begging for a new glamorie.

Well, Rook wasn't waiting around to listen to that. A stick-servant led him through the dark hallways of the nathe, then along a secret side tunnel and out a door that opened straight into the forest. In his dog shape he made it to the Lake of All Ways without any run-ins with the nathe-wardens.

Standing on the shore, the pebbles smooth and cool

under his paw pads, he sniffed the air with his long dog nose and contemplated the Lake of All Ways. Pucks traveled a lot. They had to. For one thing, they were hunted out of all the lands, so they never stayed anywhere for long. For another, they were always looking for puck babies.

That was how pucks came to be brothers. A puck was born to a fern-woman, or a couple of duck-people, or a Lady of a swampland—to anyone, really. As soon as the parents saw the black hair and flame-colored eyes and realized their new baby was a puck, they abandoned it, leaving it at a Way for other pucks to find.

Usually he and his brothers found the babies in time. Though sometimes they didn't.

At any rate, Rook knew what land the Sea-Lord lived in. He'd been there before. The Way to that land was always open. It was open now.

He might be walking into trouble where he'd need his teeth, so he stayed in his dog form. Then he stepped into the Lake, and into the Way.

As Rook came through to the Sealands, he blinked at a setting sun that blasted him straight in the eyes.

Then the smell hit him. A wave of dank stench—dead fish, dead seaweed, dead crabs and snails, all left behind by the sea and baked for days under a hot sun.

Quickly he spat out his shifter-tooth, panting. Ugh.

Too much of him was nose when he was a dog.

Covering his mouth and nose with his arm, and breathing through his coat sleeve, he surveyed the Sealands. The last time he'd been here the clouds had been gray and spitting rain into a wind-tossed sea bashing itself against sharp, black rocks. On a patch of sandy beach, sleek seals had gathered, and seabirds had wheeled in the sky, diving to pluck tiny fish from the waves.

Rook climbed from the rocky ledge where the Way opened down to the beach, where he stood looking out. The setting sun glared at him across a muddy plain edged by black rocks that were no longer wet with spray. The sea itself had receded; he saw it, flat and reflecting the bloodred sky, far out over the mud.

The plain of mud was where the death smell was coming from. It was covered with dead snails, rotting fish, strands of decaying seaweed, the empty shells of crabs. No seabirds circled overhead. All was still and silent.

Clearly something was wrong here. It must be the land's Forsworn Lord's broken oath causing it. But what was wrong, exactly?

A sandy path led from the beach. It ran parallel to the shoreline, winding around dunes covered with long, dry grass that hung limp in the still air. He followed the path, the setting sun glaring over his left shoulder, breathing shallowly to keep out the stench that hovered over the mudflats. He walked and walked; the path led on; the sun squatted on the edge of the sky.

He stopped and looked out, shading his eyes. The sun had been stuck in that spot since he'd arrived. It should be night by now. He shook his head and went on.

At last, the path came out on a wide stretch of sand. Squinting, he saw, way down the beach, a huddle of dark shapes. People, it looked like. He set off across the hard-packed sand. The sun still sat on the horizon; no wind blew. The sound of his boots scuffing on the sand sounded loud in the silence.

Finally he reached the people. They watched him come, wide, dark eyes in dark faces, then turned their heads again to stare out at the faraway sea.

They were seal-people. They had long, plump bodies and short arms and legs with webbed fingers and toes. Sleek, brown fur covered their earless heads; the men had spiky whiskers around their mouths. They sat close together, as if taking comfort from one another.

The seal-people were wildling, he realized—their Lord's broken oath was turning them into wild creatures that would soon forget that they'd ever been people. Their land was dying before their eyes. They were unbound and adrift, and they were feverish and frightened.

They might be too far gone to answer his questions.

Awkwardly Rook stepped closer and crouched next to a seal-woman. "Has your Lord been here?" he asked. His voice sounded rough and too loud.

The seal-woman looked at him. "Our Lord has gone away." Then she turned her head again to stare out at the sea.

Rook found himself staring too, and shook his head. The air was so heavy here; it made his thoughts slow. If Fer was here, she'd brew some sort of medicinal tea to help the seal-people, but there was nothing he could do for them.

The seal-woman turned her head back. When she spoke, her words were slurred, as if she had almost forgotten how to talk. "The sea comes in," she said for-lornly. "The sea goes out. Then it comes in again." She gazed out over the mud. The bloody sun was reflected in her eyes. "Then the sea went out and it never came in."

She was talking about the tide, Rook realized. The sea washing in and out according to the movement of the moon. The seal-people were waiting for the sea to come back. If the tide went out and never came in . . .

It meant the Lord's broken oath had broken something in his land. And it meant the Lord had abandoned his land and his people.

This land was stuck. The coming and going of the tides, the turning of the moon—those things were changes, part of the rhythm of the land. Because the Forsworn would not change, their lands wouldn't change either. Maybe all the lands of the Forsworn were like this. Abandoned, dying.

He looked out over the mudflats; the smell of death washed over him again. The seal-people sat, hunched and unmoving. Waiting. They would be dead soon too.

He needed to warn Fer. As a part human, she was the force of change in the lands. If anybody could do something to save the lands of the Forsworn, it was she.

But he'd been away from his brothers for too long. He needed to see them first.

Lately the pucks had made their home in a huge tree in a forest made up of other huge trees. Just the cracks in the bark of those trees were deep enough for a puck to hide in; the trees themselves were a hundred paces across, and so tall, a puck could climb up them all day long and never reach the top, and if he did, he'd find strange creatures and plants living on those high branches, and maybe strange people, too. The land of the tree-giants was rainy and damp most of the time, the ground covered with ferns and pine needles. A good place for sneaking, because no footstep ever made a sound.

The tree his brothers lived in had been struck by lightning and burned; the pucks had dug out the burned place in the base of the trunk to make a cavelike shelter with a wide opening looking out over the forest. When Rook arrived, the tree was buzzing with activity. As he padded up and shifted into his person shape, his brothers saw him. "Rook!" they shouted, and, "Brother!"

Rook grinned. It was good to be home.

Asher strode up and gave him a quick hug. "Pup!" he said, beaming. "You've come at just the right time." He grabbed Rook's arm and pulled him deeper into the hollowed-out tree. "How did the shadow-web work?" he asked.

Rook started to answer, but Asher shook his head. "Wait a moment; tell everybody." He dragged Rook to the charred back wall of the shelter, where Rip and Tatter and a few other pucks sat in a circle. They were tying thick ropes into what looked like a net. The toddler-puck, Scrap, sat on Tatter's lap; seeing Rook, Scrap grinned, showing off his new teeth. Rook grinned back at him.

"We're almost done with this, Ash," Rip said. "Hello, Pup."

Rook nodded a greeting. "What're you doing?" he asked.

"Oh, Pup," Asher said, grinning. "Just wait until you hear the next part of the plan." He pulled Rook down beside him. "But first tell us about that." He pointed at

Rook's left hand, at the bit of shadow-web still stuck to his palm.

He told them what had happened, how the Birch-Lady had shriveled up and howled in pain when the glamorie had come off her.

"Huh," Asher said. "But her glamorie was destroyed?"

"It was, yes," Rook answered. Then he realized that Rip was staring fixedly at him.

"You haven't mentioned that Lady Gwynnefar yet," Rip said.

That's because he hadn't wanted to mention her. "We're not . . ." He had to stop and clear the lump out of his throat. "We're not friends anymore, Fer and me."

"Good," Rip said, with a fierce smile. "No more thread binding you, then?"

Rook shook his head. He rubbed the place on his chest where the shards of the shattered heart-thread still poked at him.

"Ah, but he's broken up about it," Tatter said. "It's clear enough that he is."

"Just leave it," Rook muttered.

They left it.

Evening fell, and the pucks went out and built up the bonfire before the tree-cave and roasted delicious things over the flames. Rook ate his fill and then, exhausted, found a warm corner of the cave to sleep in.

In the morning, he opened his eyes to see Asher leaning against the cave wall; beside Asher stood a grinning Tatter, holding the baby Scrap.

Tatter said something. "No, he hasn't noticed it yet," Ash answered. "Pup," he said, and nudged Rook's shoulder with his toe, "come and have some tea once you're awake."

"Come have some breakfast, too, Pup," Tatter said, then went away with Ash.

Rook's bed against the wall of the tree-cave was too comfortable. He didn't want to get up. He looked at the dark curve of the cave overhead; gray light flooded in from the wide doorway. He heard a buzzing noise. Then a tickling on his chest, right over his heart. He looked down at himself and saw a bedraggled bee clinging to his fine coat, buzzing softly.

A bee?

Fer's bee.

He sat up with a jerk and the bee tumbled off, then gave an annoyed buzz and flew up to perch on his collar. "What are *you* doing here?" Rook whispered.

Hmmmzmmrm, the bee answered.

Oh, his brothers were not going to like this. Rook got to his feet and went out to the campfire in front of the cave. His brother Ash was sitting beside it, munching on a strip of dried rabbit. The other pucks lounged around on blankets, some of them sleeping in their dog shapes.

Tatter handed him a cup of hot tea. "Here, Pup," he said. "Drink this."

Rook took the cup and wrapped his fingers around it, warming them. The bee buzzed at his ear. *Hurryhurry,* he thought it meant.

"I know," he whispered. "I'll tell them in a moment."

Rip came up then. "I see our Pup has got a pet," he said darkly.

The bee, he meant. "It's Fer's," he said, though they already knew that, he guessed. "Its coming here means she's in trouble."

"What's that to us?" Rip asked.

"We thought she wasn't friends with you anymore," Ash added.

"She's not," he said. He knew Ash was watching for it, so he didn't rub at the sore place over his heart. "But she needs my help."

"*We* need your help with the next part of our plan, Pup," Asher said.

"You still haven't told me about the plan," Rook said.

Ash shrugged. "We'll get to it." His eyes narrowed as he watched Rook carefully. "Are you going to send that bee away?"

Sending the bee away meant abandoning Fer. He

couldn't do that. "She's in trouble, and I'm going to help her," he insisted. He had decided to stay true to Fer; he wasn't changing his mind about that. "I'll come back to help you as soon as I can."

Ash and Rip exchanged a glance. "All right, Brother," Ash said slowly, getting to his feet. "Do what you have to do." Then he grinned. "While you're off finding out what trouble your not-a-friend Lady Gwynnefar's gotten herself into, we'll work on the rest of our plan. But you'd better hurry, Pup," he said. "We're not going to wait forever."

twelve

The time-spell on the tower pressed down on Fer like a heavy hand. It wanted her to sit against the wall and stare at the opposite wall. Eventually she would slow, and stop, and be stuck there, alive and unmoving.

"No, I won't," Fer whispered.

Summoning up all her human strength, and all her determination, she pushed herself to her feet. She *would* find a way out of here.

She looked up. The way out was the trapdoor, high above. She had to get up there somehow.

On her hands and knees, she crawled over the stone floor of the tower searching for anything she could use to escape. On the first search she found nothing. Her knees were getting bruised from the hard floor, and her fingers grew sore from poking at the stone.

"And again," she whispered to herself. It wasn't like she had anything else to do. So she started again, this time feeling the stone walls as high as she could reach, then down to the ground.

At last, at a spot she'd been over before, where the curved wall met the floor, she found something wedged into a crack. With sore fingers she picked at it, then eased it out.

She sat back on her heels to examine what she'd found. A shard of dull-gray rock about as long as her hand, pointed at one end.

"Ha," she breathed. Take that, Forsworn. The shard wasn't as sharp as a knife, but it was sharp enough.

Climbing to her feet, she gripped the shard. At the wall, she traced the crack between two stones. The mortar cementing the stones together felt sandy under her fingers. With the sharp end of the rock, she gouged at the mortar. A little of it flaked away, chalky white and dusty. She breathed in a little of the dust, and it made her cough. She gripped the shard more tightly and attacked the mortar again.

After a long time, she'd chipped away enough mortar that the crack between the stones was exposed. Then she did another one, at the same level. Then another, higher up.

By this time, she was covered with chalky, gritty dust; her hands felt sore from gripping the shard. Her eyes burned from the dust, and from staring at the stone blocks that made up the wall. The time-spell pressed down on her, telling her to give up, to stop, to be still and silent.

Part of her felt lulled by the time-spell. It was the same part of her that wanted the summer in her own land to go on forever, never changing, golden and warm and peaceful and safe.

Another part of her—the human part, she knew—didn't want that at all. Her human part liked change and adventure, and it knew that a human life is short and the one living it had to seize every single moment before it flitted away.

That stubborn human part of her pushed the time-spell from her and kept working. *Chip, chip, chip.*

There. Time to try it. Sitting on the stone floor, she took off her sneakers and socks, then stood and stowed the rock shard in her jacket pocket. She reached and slid her fingers into the highest crack she'd made. She pulled herself up and wedged her bare toes into each of the lower cracks. She looked down. Three whole feet from the floor. She looked up. Maybe twenty more feet to go.

Determined, she reached into her pocket and pulled out the rock shard. Gritting her teeth, trying to ignore the cramps that were already setting into her fingers and toes, she chipped at the mortar in the next-highest crack between the stones. Making the next handhold, the next toehold.

And the next.

And the next.

"Never give up," she told herself, her voice raspy with powdered mortar.

And the next.

"I am human," she said, gritting her teeth. "I will *not* be trapped here."

And the next.

Chip, chip, chip.

At last, after a long weary time and many trips up and down the wall as she worked, and a shard of rock that was starting to crumble, she made one final handhold at the top of the wall. Then she climbed down to the floor. What was left of the shard she put into her pocket. She stuffed her socks into her sneakers and tied their laces together and slung them over her shoulder. The powdered mortar, she'd found, was useful; it made her fingers grip better without getting sweaty or slippery. She dusted her hands and bare feet with the powder. Then she looked up at the trapdoor, high above. This was going to take some fancy moves.

The time-spell pulled at her, making her arms and legs feel heavy and slow. It wanted her to sit down, to close her eyes, to rest.

If she did that, she knew, she'd never wake up again.

Summoning her human strength, she took a deep breath and started up the wall, pulling herself higher and higher. Her fingers knew how to cling to the cracks. She pressed herself against the wall, the stone gritty and cold under her cheek. The muscles in her forearms and calves quivered with tiredness as she pulled herself higher. At last she reached the top.

The trapdoor was in the middle of the ceiling. Too far to reach; and anyway, she couldn't let go of the wall long enough to stretch out an arm. She'd have to jump for it.

"Don't look down," she told herself. Without a pause to steady herself, she flung herself away from the wall with all her strength; at the same time she reached with her hands. The time-spell clung to her, didn't want to let her go—and then, with a snap, the spell was broken, and *there* was the edge of the trapdoor under her fingers. She clung for a moment, then hauled herself higher to get an elbow over, and she was wrenching herself out of the time-spell and up and out and lying on the roof of the tower, panting, with the rays of the setting sun slanting down.

Happiness flashed through her, and she laughed.

She'd made it! She'd actually made it out! Free of the tower and the time-spell, at last! She heard the sound of waves pounding on rocks and breathed in the briny, fishy smell of the sea. Sitting up, she looked around.

The sun was setting, dropping over the edge of a wide, green sea. She got to her feet, feeling the ache of muscles from her climb, and turned in a circle. She saw ocean in all directions. Empty ocean with no birds flying over it, no clouds in the sky, no boats bobbing on the horizon. She went to the edge of the tower and peered down.

Steps were carved into the outside of the wall; that was something. But the tower sat on a scrap of land only a little bigger than it was. There was no beach—just sharp black rocks being lashed by the waves. Her smile died on her face. She was on an island. She had nothing to eat and nothing but salt water to drink. As the sun dropped over the horizon, the wind picked up and the air grew chill.

But wait. The Forsworn had brought her here; surely there was a Way nearby. She closed her eyes and lifted her hand, trying to sense, by the tingling in her fingers, a Way.

Yes. A Way opened right here, on the tower. She reached out for it, and used her Lady's power to open it, but it stayed stubbornly closed, like a locked door. She frowned. The Forsworn must be stationed on the other side, sealing it.

The wind gusted, blowing icy spray from the rocks across the top of the tower.

Shivering, Fer sat down and put her head in her hands.

She'd escaped one prison only to find herself trapped in another.

thirteen

Leaving his brothers, Rook went through the Way on his own, following Fer's bee. It led him to a Way and across a peaceful, green land into yet another Way.

"Is this it?" Rook asked, but the bee bumbled in a circle around his head as if it was confused. The Way it wanted to go through was closed.

He frowned. It was a Way he'd used in his wanderings before, and it hadn't been closed then. The bee led him back and through three other Ways. It was as if they were taking all the back Ways the bee could find. "I should have brought some food with me," Rook complained.

Hmmmzimzum, and the bee led him into another Way, this one a wide prairie. Tall grasses waved and yellow flowers bobbed under a cloudless, late-afternoon sky. "We need to hurry," Rook said. Fer might have sent the bee days ago. With an irritated buzz, the bee shot ahead; Rook had to shift into his horse form to keep up. He and the bee raced through the dry prairie grass for long enough that the sun started sliding over the edge of the sky, toward night. As its setting beams stretched across the prairie, the bee turned and swooped back at Rook. He dodged it and dropped into a walk, then stopped, spitting out his shifter-bone. Panting, he stowed the bit of bone in the pocket of his fine, embroidered coat. "What?" he asked the bee.

Zrrrmzmzm, it answered, then darted ahead and back again so fast that Rook had to duck into the tall grass to avoid being hit.

Then he saw what the bee was pointing him toward, and telling him to hide from. Ahead was a stand of trees, darkly silhouetted against the sky where the sun had just gone down. Young oaks, it looked like. He crouched, squinting. The sky was darkening, but he thought he caught a glimpse of a thread of smoke drifting up. Yes, somebody had built a fire at the edge of the trees.

The bee wanted him to be careful. Best to wait until full night, then. He shifted into his dog shape and settled into the grasses that waved higher than his ears. As night came on, the smell of the campfire was keen in his nose, along with the fainter smell of roasted meat; whoever was over there was cooking dinner. His stomach rumbled. A nice, fresh rabbit would taste good right now.

A sliver of moon hung in the sky. It was time. Still in his dog shape, he slunk toward the trees, a shadow passing through the high grass.

As he drew closer, he realized why the bee had brought him here. A Way opened in the trees. Surely Fer was on the other side of it.

He slunk closer, then paused, belly to the ground, watching. A dark figure crossed in front of the fire. It was looking out, he realized. Straight toward where he was hiding.

A watcher. The figure said something in a low voice and was joined by three others. Guards, then. Guarding the Way.

Moving quietly, he spat out his shifter-tooth, keeping it in his hand in case he needed it fast. The bee settled on his collar, buzzing softly.

The crescent moon didn't give him much light to see by. He crawled closer, the prairie grass prickly and dryly rustling. *Shhhh,* he told it.

One of the figures had stepped away from the fire. It was glowing, he realized, with its own light.

A glamorie!

He froze. Those were Lords and Ladies, those watchers. Forsworn, no doubt. He felt a nibble of fear. If the

Forsworn had taken her, as they'd tried to do before, Fer must be in big trouble on the other side of that Way. He had to get to her, and soon.

He could try to get past them to the Way. But there were four of them, and—he saw a glint of a knife in the pale moonlight—they were armed and ready.

Slowly he rose to his feet. He heard one of the Forsworn hiss a warning to the others, and he heard the swish of an arrow being drawn from a quiver. He crouched down again.

"It must be the puck," he heard. Trying not to rustle the grass, he crept away from the spot where they'd sighted him. No point in giving them a target to shoot at.

"Don't let him touch you," one warned. "He killed Marharren with a touch of his hand."

Marharren—must be the name of the Birch-Lady. "She's not dead!" he shouted, and immediately scrambled away. Two arrows slammed into the spot where he'd just been hiding.

Good shots, these Forsworn.

"I need to get through that Way," he called, and as he leaped to the side, he felt an arrow flash past his ear. He flung himself flat onto the ground. They were Forsworn, and that meant they wouldn't hesitate to spill his blood in this land if they caught him.

This wasn't going to work. He'd have to try something else.

Silently he edged out of range of their bows, then shifted to his horse shape to gallop back to the Way he'd used to come into this land. While he ran through the high grass, as the stars climbed up into the sky, he thought about what he should do next.

He could go and ask his brothers for help, but they'd made it clear they wouldn't do anything to help Fer. He couldn't go back to the nathe; that would be to admit to Arenthiel that there was a *we*, and anyway, the nathe wasn't a good place for a puck to go unless he wanted to get reacquainted with its underground prison cells. It'd have to be the Summerlands, then, and hope that the stupid wolf-guards would listen to what he had to say before ripping his throat out.

It wasn't just a prison, Fer realized. It was a death sentence. She was on an island in the middle of a saltwater ocean. It had been a long time since her bee had flown away in search of help. Maybe nobody was coming to rescue her.

"Okay," she breathed. She would have to keep herself alive; that was all.

She went to the edge of the tower and peered over it. A narrow staircase was carved out of the rock, winding around the tower to the ground. Carefully she climbed onto the steps and edged down them. It was way easier than climbing up the inside walls of the tower, anyway.

When she reached the ground, Fer brushed off her hands and explored the island. It didn't take very long. The island was only a little wider than the tower, and covered with huge, bare black rocks. Down near the water, the rocks were encrusted with seaweed and barnacles; higher up they were dry and warm from the sun. The wind blew steadily; the sun shone down from directly overhead, leaving only a puddle of shadow around the base of the tower.

Shading her eyes, she looked out over the sea. Up close to the island, the waves were rough and edged with foam, crashing against the black rocks, throwing up spray. In the distance, the sea looked smooth, like a rippled, blue, silken cloth. She couldn't see any sign of a ship anywhere.

"That doesn't mean there aren't any ships," she told herself, needing to hear the sound of her own voice instead of the incessant rush and crash of the wind and the waves.

A fire—that's what she needed. A signal fire.

She circled the island again, finding bits of sodden driftwood wedged in cracks between the rocks, and pulling up swathes of kelp from the edge of the water.

She lay the kelp and the wood on a flat rock to dry.

Her stomach growled. "I wonder when I last ate," she said to herself. A strange bubble of laughter burst inside her, and she giggled. She wasn't happy and it wasn't funny. She was alone, and the horror of what she'd done to the Birch-Lady weighed heavy on her shoulders, but it was so weird, talking to herself like this. "Fer," she asked, "when did you last eat?" She shook her head. "I don't know, Fer," she answered.

She'd been alone in the tower for a long time. It might have been days since her last meal. "Do you want to try some kelp?" she asked herself. She picked up a strand of the drying kelp and sniffed at it. The kelp smelled like the ocean; she tasted it with the tip of her tongue: salty. "It *is* vegetarian, after all," she told herself, and the weird laugh bubbled up in her again. The kelp was rubbery and didn't really taste like anything. She ate a little, and realized that she'd made a mistake. The saltiness of it had made her thirsty, and there was nothing to drink.

She checked the driftwood. It was still damp, and even on the hot, black rocks, it wasn't getting dry. The kelp had shriveled in the hot sun, but it was damp, too.

The day was ending. The blue silk of the sea had turned bronze, with a shimmering path of gold leading to the setting sun. The sky was mostly a clear, deepening blue, with a few thin clouds at the blurred line where it arched down to meet the sea.

"Maybe it'll rain tomorrow," Fer said. Kelp wasn't very good to eat, but she could make a cup out of it, in case it really did rain.

As the sun set, she made a few bowls out of the rubbery kelp, and gouged hollows out of the spongy driftwood. When it was too dark to see, she felt her way up the stone steps to the top of the tower.

She wrapped herself in her patched jacket and lay down. Her mouth felt so dry, almost too dry to swallow. The day had been hot, but now that the sun was gone the wind felt cold as it blew over her. The sky had turned the deepest, velvety black, and the stars hung down like lanterns, so bright and close she felt as if she were floating among them.

"I haven't slept for days," she told herself, and her voice sounded creaky. She shivered under the starry sky, and after a long time she fell asleep.

fourteen

Rook crouched outside the Way that led into Fer's land, waiting for sunrise, when it would open, and picturing plump, juicy rabbits roasting over an open fire. His stomach growled, and he growled back at it. He was tired from the long run across the prairie, and he knew Fer's stupid wolf-guards were not going to listen to him. The whole situation made him cranky.

At last the sun came up. The Way opened, and he stepped through into the clearing in the Summerlands.

Rain pounded down from a gloomy sky. Rook was soaked in an instant. He pushed soggy hair out of his eyes to see, and something hit him hard from the side. Down he went, onto the sodden grass with the wolf-guard girl sitting on his chest; a fierce fox-girl grabbed each of his arms. "Get *off*," he yelled, and tried to squirm out of their grip.

The wolf bared her teeth. "Where is Ladyfer?" she snarled. "She left here with you, Puck, and she hasn't come back."

Oof, the wolf-girl was heavy. "She's in trouble," he gasped. Rain slashed into his eyes; the wolf-guard loomed over him, a dripping shadow.

"If she's in trouble, Puck, it must be your fault," the wolf-guard growled. "Come on. You're not wanted here." She climbed off him and jerked him to his feet, holding him by the front of his coat. The fox-girls were still gripping his arms. A male wolf-guard stepped up and grabbed him by the collar from behind.

"Is it biting time?" the wolf behind him asked; his breath was hot and stinky on the back of Rook's neck.

"You've been eating rabbits, haven't you," Rook gasped.

The girl wolf-guard scowled. "Yes, bite him if he gives us any trouble." She looked over her shoulder. "The Way is still open." She and the fox-girls dragged him toward it; the wolf-guard pushed. "Out you go again, Puck."

He struggled, but there were too many of them. *"No,"* he protested.

From the direction of the forest he heard a whinny; he squinted through the rain, and saw Phouka, his mane and tail bedraggled, prance into the clearing. "Brother!" he shouted.

Phouka trotted across the clearing, pushed a badger-man out of his path, and stood blocking the Way; then he gave a snort that sounded like the horse equivalent of a laugh.

Rook summoned up a grin. It *was* a little funny, after all: Fer's people trying to shove him out the Way like this, when he'd come here because their Lady needed help.

"Puck," the wolf-girl warned.

He wiped the smile from his face. "Look, you stupid wolf—" he started, growling.

No, wait. That wasn't the way to convince her. He dredged around in his memory and came up with her name. "Fray," he said. That got her attention; she leaned closer.

At that moment, Fer's bee, which had been hiding from the rain under the embroidered collar of Rook's coat, crawled out and then onto Fray's hand, where she was gripping him.

With a cry, the wolf-guard let him go; she cupped her hands and the bee sheltered inside, safe from the rain. "The Lady's bee!"

"See?" Rook asked. He glared down at the fox-girls; they glared back, but released his arms. The other wolf-guard let him go too. He shrugged his sopping-wet coat straight again. "The bee came to warn me. Your Lady is in trouble." With his wet sleeve, he swiped the rain off his face. "I can help her, but I need your help to do it."

A grumble of thunder echoed across the sky. The rain came down harder, a chilly, gray curtain. He shivered. Come *on*, Wolf.

"All right," the wolf-guard said, and nodded toward the forest. "We'll get out of the rain, and you'll tell us what's going on." Then she leaned closer to Rook and dropped her voice into a rumbling growl even lower than the thunder. "But if you are trying to trick us, Puck, you will regret it for the rest of your short and miserable life."

In the morning, Fer woke up and realized that she wasn't alone.

At the edge of the tower perched a big, gray-and-white bird.

She sat up. At her movement, the bird—a seagull, Fer realized—fluttered its wings, but then it settled down again. It looked bedraggled; its feathers were ruffled, as if it had been flying for a long time. Maybe the steady wind had blown it here.

"Hello," Fer said, rubbing the sleep out of her eyes.

The seagull cocked its head and looked at her out of one beady, golden eye.

Fer's stomach growled. "I'm hungry," she told the seagull.

She straightened her patched jacket, combed her short hair with her fingers, and climbed down the narrow steps to the ground. To her surprise, the seagull swooped down to perch on a rock next to her.

"You're somebody to talk to, anyway," Fer said. Her mouth felt even drier than it had the day before. Her stomach growled again, like a deep, empty pit. The kelp was not going to be much of a breakfast.

She eyed the seagull. It eyed her back. "Don't worry," she said. "I'm not going to eat you."

If Rook were here, she found herself thinking, he'd want to eat the seagull.

"No," she told herself. "I'm not going to think about Rook." Or the dead Lady, or any of that. The only thing she had to focus on was surviving this prison.

In the tower, she'd found the shard of rock, and that had saved her. Maybe she'd missed something when she first explored the island. She went over every inch of ground again, followed by the curious seagull, looking for something that might help her. Halfway through the morning, she crawled down to the lower part of the island, where the waves flung themselves onto the rocks and then sucked back in a foaming rush. All along the edge of the sea was seaweed and, clinging to the rocks, clusters of sleek, black mussels. As a wave washed out, Fer edged down, ripped up a handful of the mussels, and retreated to the higher rocks. The mussels felt cold and heavy, and were covered with seaweed that looked like moss. She set them down on a patch of warm rock.

The seagull hopped up beside her.

Fer licked her lips. She was *so* thirsty, and so hungry. If she smashed the shells open, the mussels might be juicy and delicious. But . . .

Mussels didn't have eyes or brains, and they weren't like cows or pigs or chickens, but they were meat. She knew what Grand-Jane would have to say about that—and at the thought of her grandmother she felt a sudden, fierce pang of lonesomeness that made a sob catch at her throat. No tears, though; her eyes were too dry.

The seagull reached down with its long, yellow beak and tapped at one of the mussels.

Fer sighed. "You're right," she croaked. "I'm not going to eat these." Anyway, it was water she needed most, not food. She gathered them up in her hands and tossed them back onto the rocks at the edge of the island.

By afternoon, her stomach had stopped growling. Her mouth felt like it was full of sand. "I'd better stay out of the sun," she whispered. And out of the wind, which blew and blew without stopping. The seagull hunched and turned its beak into that wind, looking like an old man wearing a gray raincoat.

Fer huddled in the shadow of the tower. As the sun marched across the sky, the shadow moved, and she moved with it.

Nobody was coming. The bubbles of laughter were all gone. Her eyes felt gritty and her mouth felt as dry as paper. Her words were drying up too.

fifteen

The Summerlands had moved well into autumn since Rook had left with Fer. The rain had thinned to a chilly drizzle, and fog crept in among the roots and dying ferns. In the gray air, the red and yellow and orange leaves of the trees glowed like a banked fire in a bed of ashes. The leaves of the Lady Tree, a huge, silver-barked beech tree, were a deep purple brown; raindrops dripped from every twig.

Rook crouched just inside the door of Fer's house in the Lady Tree's branches. A cold breeze blew in from outside, but he didn't want to go farther into the room, where it was warmer. His brother Phouka was on the ground below the Tree, waiting. Across the room were Fer's most trusted people, all frowning and ranked against him and disbelieving every word that he said, curse them. Up where the roof peaked overhead, the rest of Fer's bees hovered in a grumbling swarm.

He shivered and his stomach growled, the sound loud in the silence. A few last drops of rain spattered on the roof.

He had told them about what had happened at the nathe, how he and Fer had made the mistake with the Birch-Lady's glamorie. He held up his hand and they'd edged closer to look suspiciously at the bit of shadow-web that was etched across his palm. He didn't tell them about how Fer had broken the thread that had connected them, but he did tell how Fer had left, and then how her bee had found him.

"It's a good story," the wolf-guard Fray said, frowning. "I'm not sure I believe it."

The bee had settled on his collar again. *Zmmmzim-zimrm,* it buzzed.

"See?" Rook said, pointing at it. "The bee says I'm telling the truth."

Fray shook her head. "Only the Lady can understand the bees, you lying puck."

Really? "Why are you talking to me, then, bee?" he asked it.

The bee gave a smug buzz.

Curse it. "Look," he said to Fer's people. "Night is

coming. When the Way opens, I'm going through it whether you are with me or not, and I'm going back to another Way that is guarded by the Forsworn, because Fer is on the other side of it. Maybe I'll get through, or maybe they'll kill me, but I'm going."

Their grim faces watched him.

"I need your help," he finished, "if you'll give it to me." As he spoke, he realized how unlikely that would be. A Lady's people, helping a puck. It'd never happen. He'd have to go stupidly die trying to get Fer out of whatever trouble she was in, and maybe she would die too.

"Idiots," he muttered. Wearily he got to his feet and went out, then climbed down a rope ladder to the ground, where Phouka was waiting.

He leaned against the rough bark of the tree; his brother nudged him in the shoulder with his nose. "D'you suppose they've got any rabbits around here?" he asked.

Phouka gave his snorting laugh.

"Fine for you," Rook grumbled. "You eat grass."

He could eat grass too, in his horse shape. But rabbits were better. He tossed his shifter-tooth under his tongue and shifted into his dog shape, and went out to hunt for something juicy and long-eared and delicious to eat.

Later, as the day grew darker, he loped to the Way, ready to head out and set himself up as a target for Forsworn arrows. At least he'd be full of rabbit when they got him; that was something.

As he entered the clearing, his ears twitched; he shifted into his person shape and cocked his head, listening. Then, from behind, came Fer's bees in a glittering swarm. They swooped past and spun into a buzzing whirlwind all around him. Then they hovered over his head as if waiting.

They *were* waiting.

"You're coming?" he asked.

Their answer was a muted roar of a buzz—*yes*, it meant.

"You *are* talking to me," Rook muttered. That didn't make any sense at all.

From behind him came the sound of heavy footsteps in the misty woods; he turned to see the wolf-guard Fray; she had a long knife sheathed at her waist. With her came one of the twin fox-girls—Twig, he thought it was—and following them came Phouka.

Fray strode to the middle of the clearing, a few paces from where the Way would open, and folded her arms. "We're going to save our Lady," she said. "But you're coming with *us*, Puck; we're not going with *you*. Understand? The bee made a mistake. It should have come to us. We're in charge. We're giving the orders."

"And you—" The tiny fox-girl narrowed her eyes and folded her arms just like the much larger wolf-girl. "You're obeying the orders."

"Oh, sure," Rook said warily.

"All right, then," Fray said.

"All right," the fox-girl echoed.

They stood in silence, waiting for the Way to open. Phouka stamped impatiently. The bees hovered over Rook's head; the one bee was clinging to his coat collar. His clothes were still damp from the rain; as the night drew on the air grew colder, and he started shivering. He'd shift into his dog shape for its warm fur, except that he had to tell them some things.

"Look, Fray," he started.

"We don't want to talk to you, Puck," the wolf-guard said, staring straight ahead.

"Just listen, then." He kept going before she could tell him to stop. "We could have a problem when we get to the Way I told you about." He'd had time during the long afternoon to think it through. It was going to be tricky. He'd have his teeth and fierceness in his dog form, and Phouka could fight, and the bees might be even better allies. Fray and the fox-girl were loyal to Fer—and Fer was loyal to them—but if there was any fighting . . .

"Those Forsworn I was telling you about," he went on. "The ones guarding the Way where Fer is. They're Lords and Ladies, and they're wearing glamories. They might be hard to resist."

The wolf-guard gave a sharp nod; she and the fox-girl exchanged a glance. "Fer is our Lady, and she's sworn to us, too," Fray said gruffly. "We won't be ruled by anyone, especially not these Forsworn ones."

Good. But they'd still have to be careful.

At last the long afternoon ended; the sun went down behind the heavy clouds, and the Way opened. They followed the bee through the winding trail of Ways until they came to the Way that led to the prairie land. They went through that wide-open Way . . .

And walked straight into an ambush.

The bees gave the first warning, shooting ahead as Rook stepped into the long prairie grass with the wolf-girl beside him and Phouka and the fox-girl, Twig, right behind. An arrow scraped across Phouka's shoulder, and he whinnied and shoved past Rook as he shied away.

"Get down!" Rook shouted, and pulled Fray with him as he fell. Arrows whizzed over their heads. He peered through the waving grasses. Thirty paces away, the Forsworn were lined up, tall and proud; one of them, a delicate bird-man, pulled another arrow from his quiver and gracefully pulled back his bow, ready to shoot; two of the others held long knives, the fourth a drawn bow.

If only Fer were with them, Rook found himself thinking—she was as good an archer as they were.

The glamories of the Forsworn were dazzling under the brilliant sun and the clear, blue sky. They were too bright, really. More dazzling than a glamorie should be. Rook blinked away the glare and with his puck-vision caught a glimpse of the ancient creatures cowering behind the blaze of beauty.

"Now what?" Fray asked.

"I thought you were giving the orders," Rook muttered. He glanced back. The Way out of the prairie lands stood open fifteen paces behind them, a wide space shimmering among the waving grasses and flowers. Phouka had galloped out of range of the Forsworns' arrows; Twig crouched next to Fray, her sharp teeth bared, as if she was ready to fight. The bees hovered in a buzzing cloud just overhead. "I think we can fight them," he answered. It'd have to be the bees that gave them a chance. "If we—" he started, but the Forsworn interrupted.

"Give the puck to us," one of the Forsworn Lords shouted. "Give him to us, you Summerkin, and we'll give you your Lady and let you go." He stepped closer; the other Forsworn, a Lord and two Ladies, started to glide sideways through the grass, surrounding them.

Fray turned to Rook, frowning.

He could practically *see* her deciding to hand him over. "They're lying," he whispered. "They are not going to let Fer out of wherever they've put her."

"You don't know that, Puck," Fray growled back.

"You idiot!" he snarled. "They're Forsworn." He gripped her shoulder and gave her a little shake. "Their glamories are hiding their lies from you. We have to fight them!"

Fray blinked and shoved his hand away. The fox-girl edged closer, watching Rook with sharp eyes.

Before the wolf-guard could make her decision, the bees made their move. With a shrieking buzz they broke away from where they'd been hovering over Rook's head and shot through the air like golden arrows, straight toward the Forsworn.

"Come on!" Rook shouted, and as he leaped to his feet, he shifted into his dog shape and charged. He took a bound and felt an arrow flit past him, and caught a quick glimpse of Fray and Twig following him, Fray drawing her long knife from its sheath.

Hopefully they were coming to help, not grab him for the Forsworn.

Rook leaped past an archer cowering from a swarm of bees and, ducking a slash from a Lord's knife, bore him to the ground, snarling—but, keeping his promise to Fer, he was careful not to touch him with the forepaw that had the shadow-web stuck to it. Quickly he shifted into his person shape and the Lord rolled him over in the long grass and raised his knife to stab. Rook laughed and popped the shifter-bone into his mouth, and the Lord dropped the knife to dodge Rook's flailing horse hooves as he scrambled to stand on his four legs.

In a flash, Rook shifted again to his person shape and picked up the long knife. Panting, he held it up to the Lord's throat. "Hold," he shouted. The Lord froze, still kneeling on the ground. With a wild glance over his shoulder, Rook saw that Fray and Twig each had a Lord or Lady at bay, and Phouka stood over the fourth Forsworn with a hoof on her chest. The bees swooped around them, buzzing and bright against the blue sky. He shot them a fierce grin. They'd won.

Now it was time to go get Fer.

sixteen

Fer had run out of time. Her throat was dry; her lips were dry and cracked; her eyes felt like they were full of sand, and whirling sparks kept creeping in at the edge of her vision. Her hands, when she looked at them, looked bony, and when she pinched the skin on the backs of them, it felt papery under her fingers. Her head pounded, and she felt sleepy. Somehow she couldn't seem to think straight.

The seagull had disappeared. It had flown away to a better island, Fer guessed, where there was food and water to drink. The whole day she had been keeping to the tower's shadow while the brassy sun blazed down, watching for a ship on the horizon, or a rain cloud, or *something* that never came.

As night fell—her last night, she thought dizzily—she dragged herself up the narrow stone steps that wound around to the top of the tower. The Way opened there. Maybe the Forsworn would unseal it and come back for her before it was too late. Maybe her bee had found its way to the Summerlands and would bring Fray and Twig in time to save her.

Or maybe she didn't deserve to be saved. Sorrow about the death of the Birch-Lady gnawed at her with needle teeth—it was even worse than the hunger, the thirst.

She stretched herself out on the roof, clinging to the last warmth of the sun that radiated from the stones. Soon it would be gone and the cold would set in.

A full moon climbed into the sky. From where she lay, the ocean was a blurry, dark plain reflecting light in a shimmering path to the moon. The chill breeze blew over her, but she felt hot inside. Fever, the healer in her realized. Shivering, she curled into a tight ball and closed her eyes. She felt like crying, but she didn't have any tears left in her.

After a long time she heard noises. Voices lapped at her ears like waves, making words she couldn't understand. She cracked her eyes open. A shadow crouched beside her. It said something that sounded urgent, talking to somebody else. The figure shifted and the moon shone down over its shoulder, and she thought she saw . . .

"Rook?" she croaked.

In the moonlight his eyes were smudged with weariness and his face was crossed with shadows. She thought she saw him frown, and his mouth moved as if he was saying something to her. Then he was gone, or maybe she'd just imagined him, and Fray was there, a solid, safe presence. She felt Fray's strong arms under her back and knees, lifting her up. Then there was the swift wind of a passage through a Way and she fell down into a darkness so deep she thought she'd never find the bottom of it.

She came back to herself a long time later. It was the same dream she'd had before, that she was in the Lady Tree and it was rocking in the wind, only this time when she opened her eyes she saw the familiar wooden walls of her house in the Lady Tree with the rich blue-and-green fish carpet on the floor, and her chest of clothes, and sitting on a stool beside her bed, a puck with shaggy, black hair, his head bent so she couldn't see his face.

Rook was her first thought, and her stomach lurched, but no, he was older and bigger, and then he looked up and she recognized Tatter's yellower eyes, and skin the red-brown color of oak leaves in the autumn. Back when she'd healed Arenthiel after his defeat, Tatter had been the one to help her.

He cocked a grin at her and leaned back to call out the door. "Your Lady's awake, Fray." Then he leaned closer to look her in the face. "Feeling wretched, are you?" he asked. He lay a gentle hand on her forehead.

Her head ached a little, but she felt surprisingly comfortable. It was so, so good to be back in her own land. She had been parched, but now she felt like a tree whose roots were plunging into the earth and drinking deeply of the water. She gave him a wan smile.

Then she remembered the dead Birch-Lady, and her happiness dried up. She was back in the world now, and would have to face the consequences of what she'd done. Like the broken friendship with Rook, this was another thing that could never be fixed. She sighed.

Tatter had bent to pick up a mug from the floor. He straightened. "See if you can take a bit more of this." He held the cup to her lips and she drank. Bitter yarrow sweetened a bit with elderflower. Just what she'd give a patient suffering from a fever and from being stranded on an island for however many days it had been.

Fray came in then, with a tray holding a jar of honey and a spoon. Seeing Fer awake, she shoved the tray at Tatter and rushed to kneel at her bedside. "Fer!"

"Fray," Fer said. Talking was hard, but she had to get it out. "You saved my life. Thank you."

Behind her, Tatter raised his eyebrows; she saw Fray

glance over her shoulder at him and then she flushed. "No, it wasn't us, Ladyfer," she admitted. "I was there, and so was Twig, but it was that puck who saved you."

So she *had* seen Rook at the tower.

Fray leaned closer. "Lady," she whispered. "Why did you send your bee to him instead of to us?"

But she hadn't, had she? She thought back. She'd been in the tower and she'd asked the bee to go to her true friends. Why had it gone to Rook? And if it had, why had he come to save her? With the death of the Birch-Lady he had betrayed her—again—and she had broken the thread that had connected them; they were not friends anymore.

She shook her head. "The bee made a mistake, Fray," she answered weakly. "Tell me what happened."

Fray told her how Rook—*that puck*, she called him—had come to the Summerlands and after what she called *some discussion*—Fer guessed it had involved more than just talking—that Fray and Twig had agreed to go with Rook to rescue Fer, and how the bees had come too, and Phouka, then how they'd fought through the Forsworn to the Way, and how they'd had to let the Forsworn go so they could get to the tower island, where they'd found Fer nearly dead, and how the puck had shifted into a horse and galloped ahead with her to the Summerlands.

"Then the puck went off to fetch this other

puck"—Fray nodded at Tatter—"because he's a healer."
Then she added darkly, "Or so he says."

"So Rook is here?" Fer asked.

"No, Lady," Fray answered. She shrugged. "He's gone
off somewhere."

"That's our Rook," Tatter put in. "He's a wanderer."

Fer would have nodded agreement, but her eyelids felt
so heavy. Oh, Tatter had put valerian in the tea, hadn't
he, to make her sleepy. She fought it for moment, wanting to ask one more question, but then she forgot what
the question was and tumbled back into the darkness.

seventeen

Rook felt like he'd been running for days, but he didn't have time to rest. After leaving Fer at the Summerlands, he'd fetched his brother Tatter to look after her, which had taken some arguing, first with his brothers and then with Fer's people, who didn't want a *nasty puck* looking after their Lady, even if he was a healer.

Then he'd left the Summerlands again, and he was in a hurry.

When leading him to Fer, the bee had taken him to Ways that should have been open, but were closed. The pucks knew all the Ways: the ones that were open, and others that were only open at certain times. He'd never known so many Ways to be closed, though. Something was wrong about that. It must have something to do with the Forsworn.

In his dog shape, he retraced the route the bee had used when taking him to the prairie land. It led through a land of stony, dry desert, through a Way that should have led to a land of rolling, grassy hills dotted with knobs of rock; after that land came the prairie land. He loped along a rutted, rocky path and came up to that Way—he'd just passed through it the day before with Fray and Twig, and he'd come back through it in his horse form, carrying Fer to the Summerlands.

He shifted to his person shape and stepped into the Way.

It flung him back, like running into a stone wall. He landed in a heap on the rocky path. Climbing painfully to his feet, he stepped closer to the Way and raised his hand to open it, but it stayed closed.

"Locked," said a timid voice from behind him.

He jerked around. Two mouse-boys with twitchy noses and smooth, brown hair peered from behind a cairn of piled stones.

Rook narrowed his eyes, looking at them with his puck-vision. Their noses were too sharp; their hair was too much like a mouse's pelt. They were in the early stages of wildling, both of them.

"It's a puck," he heard one of them whisper.

They cowered away.

"No, wait," Rook said. "Why is this Way closed? Do you know?"

"We want to go home," one mouse-boy said. "But it's locked."

"Our Lord closed it," the other said. "Then he went away."

"He is afraid," the first mouse-boy said. "So he left us, and he left the land."

A Lord, afraid? A Lord leaving his land and his people to fend for themselves? "What's he afraid of?" Rook asked, stepping closer to the mouse-boys.

They ducked behind the cairn. "Leave us alone, Puck!" one of them squeaked.

"I'm not doing anything," Rook protested. He crouched and tried softening his voice. Mouse-people were well known for their timidity. "Why has your Lord closed the Way leading into his land? Why has he abandoned you?"

"He's afraid," one mouse-boy said.

Yes, they'd said that already. "Why, *exactly*?" he asked.

"The stillness," the other added. "The stilth. It creeps from land to land. It's coming."

Rook stood; the suddenness of his movement made the mouse-boys skitter away, squeaking. The *stillness*. Or the *stilth*, as the mouse had called it. He frowned. He'd seen the Sealands of the Forsworn Sea-Lord. That Lord's broken oath had made time stop in his land. The rhythms of the land were broken too. If that's what the stilth was—if the stillness and broken time caused by the broken oaths was spreading through the Ways—then yes, it made sense that the other Lords and Ladies were afraid and closing the Ways. But it didn't make sense that the Lords and Ladies were abandoning their lands. They were the pucks' enemies, and they wore glamories and were false liars, but the Lords and Ladies really were connected to their lands. Even a puck had to admit that at a time like this, the lands and people needed their Lords and Ladies.

Meanwhile, if the stilth spread through the Ways, it would mean silence and stillness would come to all the lands; it would mean nothing would change ever again. It would mean death for everyone.

He rubbed at the bit of shadow-web stuck to his palm and stared at the rocky ground. He wasn't sure what to do. Fer needed to know about this, and she was the obvious person to deal with this problem, but she was sick in bed in the Summerlands. His brothers—yes, he really needed to tell them what was going on. But first . . .

He sighed. Arenthiel had asked him to come back to the nathe and tell him what he discovered about the effect of the broken oaths of the Forsworn. Now he had to admit it—he'd have to take his chances with the nathe-wardens because he needed to tell Old Scrawny what he knew before he could decide what to do next.

He found his Way to the Lake of All Ways outside the nathe. Usually the pebbly shore of the Lake was deserted, its gray water still, the wide lawns outside the nathe-wall empty. This time he stepped through the Way into a crowd.

On the banks of the Lake, tents had been set up made of wool or silk or scraped hide. Outside the tents clusters of people were huddled around campfires or standing, staring at the Lake as if waiting for something.

As he crossed the shore, his feet crunching loudly on the pebbles, a group of six skunk-people with white stripes in their black hair cowered away from him. He stepped closer. "What're you doing here?" he asked.

The skunk-people held bundles or had knapsacks slung on their backs. They didn't answer, just gazed at him with wide, frightened eyes. A few of them, he realized, were wildling, just like the mouse-boys.

"Is your Lord or Lady one of the Forsworn?" he asked.

One of the skunk-people, a girl taller and bolder than the others, shook her head. "He is not, Puck. But the Way to our land is closed and our Lady has left us, and we're afraid."

"So you've come here," Rook finished for her. Maybe they thought being at the nathe would protect them. He surveyed the tents, the crowds of people. Refugees, all of them. Abandoned by their Lords or Ladies.

He left them, crossing the lawn, then climbing the gray vine-wall that enclosed the forest surrounding the nathe. Once he was on the other side, he shifted into his dog shape, wanting his sharp ears to listen for prowling nathe-wardens.

He padded through the forest. Time moved slowly here. The High Ones themselves were timeless; change never came to the place where they lived. The forest felt ancient and heavy with the weight of time. It made the fur stand up on the back of Rook's neck. Keeping his ears pricked, he made his way to the secret entrance that Arenthiel's stick-person servant had shown him.

When he slunk inside the nathe, it was strangely quiet. No nathe-wardens accosted him as he padded through its tunnel-like halls. People were there, though. His dog nose could smell them. His ears twitched, catching the slithering sound of hurrying footsteps on the polished floor, or the swish of a gown as somebody scurried away. He caught glimpses of Lords watching him from cracked-open doors; he saw Ladies peer from around corners and then disappear.

The Lords and Ladies who were abandoning their lands were coming here, to the nathe. To hide. While their people had gathered at the Lake, waiting and wildling.

It made him want to bare his teeth at them and growl.

When he reached Arenthiel's door, he shifted to his person shape and then, without knocking, he went in. An ancient creature made of gnarled bark and root and wearing a dress of withered yellow leaves sat huddled on the green cushions. On a low table before it, tea was laid out, with fine silver cups and plates of sliced fruit. Seeing him, the creature shrieked and skittered sideways off the couch, landing in a flustered heap on the floor. "The puck!" it wailed.

"I didn't do anything this time, either," Rook muttered.

One of the stick-people stuck its green-tufted head through the other doorway.

Rook nodded to it. "I need to talk to Old Scrawny."

The stick-person bowed, and popped out.

Ignoring the ancient creature behind the cushions, Rook went to the table, crouched, and poured himself a cup of mint tea. With a snap, he gobbled up three apple slices.

The door opened, and Arenthiel hobbled into the room. "Robin!" he exclaimed.

His mouth full, Rook nodded to him.

"I see you're taking tea with Marharren, the Birch-Lady," Aren said, pointing to the ancient creature, who was still crouched beside the cushion she'd fallen from.

Rook blinked. He hadn't recognized her. He lifted his hand to greet her, then realized it was his left hand with the shadow-web stuck to it, and shoved it into his pocket. Instead he nodded to her, too. Then he washed down the last bite of apple with a gulp of tea and sat on the floor. Old Scrawny settled himself on the cushions; after a moment, the Birch-Lady climbed onto the couch beside him.

Arenthiel beckoned to a stick-servant. "You'd better bring some more things to eat," he told it. Then he glanced at Rook. "Be sure some of the pastries have meat in them." Arenthiel's toothless mouth widened into a grin. "It's lovely to see you again, Robin."

Rook blinked. Nobody talked that way to a puck. But Arenthiel seemed to really mean it. And, Rook knew, Arenthiel would help him if he asked for it. "You already know my name," he said. Fer had said it in front of Arenthiel plenty of times. "You might as well call me by it."

"Oh!" Arenthiel clasped his hands together. "You honor me, Rook," he said, then cackled.

"Leave it," he growled, regretting it already. "I want to talk to you." First he told Arenthiel how Fer had been kidnapped by the Forsworn and imprisoned in a tower.

"You rescued her?" Arenthiel interrupted. When Rook nodded, Arenthiel beamed. "Then she'll know she can trust you—she'll know you're staying true!"

Rook shrugged. "She's saved my life five times,

Scrawny. Me saving her once isn't enough." Then he told Arenthiel about what he'd found in the Sealands— the sun standing on the horizon, the smell of death from the mudflats, the wildling seal-people waiting for a sea that wasn't coming back.

"Oh, that is very bad," Arenthiel mused. "Certainly caused by the Forsworn Lord of the Sealands' broken oath." He glanced aside at the Birch-Lady. "I do wonder if the same kind of broken time is affecting your land, Marharren, even though your glamorie is gone and you've fulfilled your oath."

She shrugged with a quivering of leaves.

Arenthiel leaned forward to whisper to Rook. "She didn't give up the glamorie willingly, so we can't know for sure until somebody goes to her land to find out." He nodded meaningfully.

Rook knew what that meant—he was supposed to go and spy out what was happening in her land. Not likely. He felt a growl building in his chest. "*Somebody* shouldn't go to her land, Scrawny. *She* should go."

Instead of answering, the Birch-Lady sat there and shivered like a withered tree in a winter breeze.

He glared at her. "Your people and your land need you."

"Look at me, Puck," she quavered. She looked weak, but her eyes were malevolent. "What you did to me. I cannot rule them as I am. They will not welcome me."

"You were that way before," he said ruthlessly. "Any puck could see it. You just hid it with your lying glamorie."

"Heh," Arenthiel put in. "He's right, you know, Marharren."

"Fer's right about rule, too," Rook went on. "Lady Gwynnefar, I mean. You don't need to rule your people and your land. They need you, and you should serve them."

She didn't answer, just hunched into herself and closed her eyes.

Stupid. The glamories must freeze their brains, too, so they couldn't think.

At that moment, the stick-person brought in more food and tea. Rook picked out the meatiest things and put them on a plate. All the running around had made him ravenous.

"The broken time in the Sealands isn't the only thing," Rook said, after he'd eaten two more pastries. "I talked to some mouse-people who are calling the effect of the Forsworns' broken oath the *stilth*. They said their Lord is afraid this stilth is spreading."

Aren's eyes widened. "Spreading?" he breathed. "Oh, dear. It's worse than I expected."

"That's not all," Rook added. He shot an extra glare

at the Birch-Lady. "Out of fear of the stilth, some of the Lords and Ladies are closing the Ways and abandoning their lands and their people. They're hiding here, at the nathe."

"Yes, my servants tell me what's going on in the nathe. I knew they were coming here," Aren said grimly. "But I did not know why. With the Ways closed and the Lords and Ladies in hiding, the lands will be defenseless and divided from one another. That is bad. But if this stilth is spreading through the Ways from one land to another . . ." He shook his head. "Very bad," he muttered. "Very, very bad."

Rook wrapped his arms around his bent knees. He remembered the seal-people, staring forlornly out to sea. Thinking about them felt strange. Like a gnawing at his heart. "Is there anything we can do about the stilth?" he asked.

"*We*, is it?" Arenthiel said with a sudden, toothless grin.

Rook narrowed his eyes.

"Right, right!" Arenthiel said quickly. "That is the question, isn't it." He rocked back and forth on the cushion, thinking. "Maybe nothing can be done," he murmured, as if to himself. "That would really end it all, wouldn't it?" Arenthiel frowned, and for an instant Rook caught a glimpse of . . . was it power? Something ancient, anyway, or outside the flow of time. Maybe Arenthiel really was kin to the High Ones, as he claimed.

Arenthiel rocked some more, then seemed to shake himself and nodded at Rook. "Well, it's clear enough to me, young Rook. If there is anything to be done, it has to be your Lady, Fer, who does it. For one thing, the broken oaths of the Forsworn were sworn to her, so she is the one who must see that they are mended. For another, she is part human. I don't know how much you know about humans, but they are very different from us. Time passes quickly in their lands; they are always changing. Humans are, in themselves, forces of change and creatures of time. If anyone can stop the stilth from spreading, it is Fer, with your help, if you'll give it to her."

"Yes, but *how*?" Rook asked. "We know we can't force them to give up their glamories. What are we supposed to do?"

"*I* don't know," Arenthiel said. "There must be a way. You'll have to figure that out yourselves."

"A lot of help you are," Rook grumbled.

Old Scrawny grinned. "You'd better get on with it, my dear Rook."

Rook nodded and got wearily to his feet. What he really wanted was a nap; instead he left the nathe and went to the Lake of All Ways. First he had to check to see how Fer was doing. And he needed to see how far into the lands the stilth had spread. And he'd promised his brothers, too, that he'd come back. They'd be impatient, waiting for him.

Truly, he might never sleep again.

eighteen

This time when Fer woke up, it was dark except for a lantern set on her box of clothes and turned low. A brazier piled with glowing coals sat in the corner, warming her little house. Shadows gathered at the peak of the roof and in the corners where the ceiling met the walls.

Somebody was sitting on the floor, a dark head leaning against her bed. Not Tatter this time. She shifted to the side to see who it was. Rook, sound asleep. Seeing him made an ache in her heart where she'd broken their friendship.

He'd come back from his wanderings, had he? Why was he *here*?

She'd have to wait until he woke up to ask him.

For a long time she stared up at the ceiling, letting

the guilt about the Birch-Lady nibble at her. After a while she remembered the question she'd had while falling asleep: How much time had passed while she'd been stuck in the time-spelled tower? It was fall here, even late fall, the doorstep of winter. Which meant a lot of time had passed in the human world. It might have been months since she'd last visited Grand-Jane.

She would have to deal with the Forsworn—she knew that much—and with the fact that she and Rook had killed the Birch-Lady. But first she had to go check on her grandma. After all, she had promised, and promises like that were binding.

That meant the sooner she was on her feet, the better. With shaking hands, she pushed back the blue, woolen coverlet and dragged herself up so she was sitting. Her head spun.

"What are you doing?" came a rough voice from beside her bed.

She steadied herself and looked up. "Hello, Rook," she croaked.

He rubbed his eyes. "You're supposed to be resting."

When he pointed at the bed, she saw the black smudge of the shadow-web that crossed his palm. It made her shiver, reminding her of the death of the Birch-Lady.

Rook straightened. "I'll fetch Tatter."

"No, wait," she said.

151

Grand County Middle School
Media Center
Moab, Utah 84532

He gave a half shrug and stayed where he was. He still looked tired, she noted. "Thanks for saving my life," she said.

His only answer was a wary nod.

She wasn't sure what to make of him. The thread of friendship that had tied them together had been broken three times. He'd broken it twice, and she'd broken it the third time, and it wasn't something that could be mended. Still, he was here, and he knew things that she needed to know too.

"Tell me about the Forsworn," she said.

"Oh, right," he said. "I meant to have Tatter tell you." The flames in his eyes leaped. "The Birch-Lady isn't dead. Old Scrawny cleaned the glamorie muck off her, and she was all right. She's with him at the nathe."

"Not dead," Fer repeated. She felt as if something knotted inside her had been loosened. A half laugh, half sob welled up in her throat. "And there I was," she said, her voice shaking, "thinking I deserved to be locked up in that tower for what I did."

He held up his shadow-web hand. "What *I* did, Fer," he said quietly. "I didn't tell you about what happened to the moon-spinner spider. I promised not to use the web, but I did." He bent his head so she couldn't see his face. "It wasn't meant as a betrayal."

She stared at the top of his shaggy head. What could

she say to him? It was too late for their friendship. Did his words even matter?

She wasn't sure. It was easier, for now, to change the subject. "Um, what about the Forsworn, then?"

He nodded and then told her about something called the *stilth* that might be spreading from the lands of the Forsworn, and how the Lords and Ladies of other lands were starting to close their Ways and abandon their lands for fear of it.

"The stilth is really bad, Fer," Rook finished. He'd gotten to his feet and stood staring down at the floor as he talked, with his hands shoved into the pockets of his embroidered coat.

The *stilth*, as he called it, sounded terrible. It made sense that the lands of the Forsworn ones were stuck in this kind of stillness. They rejected change, so their lands didn't change. But for the stilth to spread to other lands—that was a disaster. With a shiver, she realized that this stilth might come to her own land too.

"What about your brothers?" she asked. They were the ones Rook had betrayed her for—again—when they'd sent him to test his shadow-web on the glamorie; they were involved in this, somehow. "What are they up to?"

He shrugged and kept his head down. "They're planning something. I think they won't tell me the rest of the plan because they think I'll tell you about it." He hunched his shoulders and muttered something else.

"What did you say?" she pushed.

He gave her a quick, flame-eyed glance. "They're right. I would tell you if I knew."

She frowned. Before, Rook had always put his brothers first. Was he saying that he would put her first, for once? But how could he, without their bond of friendship?

She was starting to get sleepy again. She eased herself back onto her pillow and stared up at the shadowed ceiling. "Rook, somehow I have to deal with the Forsworn and the stilth. But first I have to talk to Grand-Jane." Her grandmother might not know how to stop the stilth, but she was all human, and even just talking to her would help Fer to figure out what she had to do. Time passed so slowly in the human world that she'd be gone from this world for only a few moments; she could take the time that she needed. "Anyway," she went on, "I promised Grand-Jane I wouldn't stay away for this long."

"Fine," Rook said sharply. "Then I'm coming with you."

No, she wanted to say. The human world made him sick if he stayed in it too long. And it would just be a quick visit. And they weren't friends anymore. But she was too sleepy. She heard his footsteps going out before she could tell him not to come.

In the end it was three more days before she was well enough to go through the Way to the human world. From her bed she used her Lady's connection to her land and sent her awareness out to sense if the stilth had come into the Summerlands. Her land hovered on the edge of winter—a bleak, quiet time—but though it felt still, it didn't feel *wrong*.

Rook disappeared for the first two days—spying out the other lands, Tatter told Fer before he pronounced her well and left to go back to his brother-pucks.

Tatter hadn't said, but she guessed Rook was meeting with his brother-pucks too, to help them with their plan, whatever it was. He stayed away from her, Fer felt sure, because he didn't want her asking him questions that he'd have to lie to answer.

Still, he was waiting for her by the moon-pool when she came up to it. She didn't bother arguing with him about whether or not he was coming with her through the Way to the human world.

"Hello, Rook," Fer said quietly. The one bee she'd brought with her lifted from her collar and buzzed a happy circle around Rook's head, and then came back.

He gave her an uncertain grin. "Think she'll be glad to see me?"

That's right, he'd spent some time with Grand-Jane,

hadn't he, when Arenthiel had sent him through the Way to die in the human world. She shook her head. "I don't know," she answered. Grand-Jane had never approved of pucks; specifically, she'd never approved of Rook.

It was the middle of a gray afternoon. The leaves of the trees around the moon-pool clearing were brown, and shivered in the breeze. Fer thought she felt a bit of winter in the wind; she hunched into her patchwork jacket, then bent to touch the moon-pool. Her fingertips tingled and the Way opened. She stepped through, Rook a half step behind her, and tumbled into the human world.

On the bank of the moon-pool she climbed to her feet.

Here in the human world it was late afternoon on a day of full summer. The stream was just a trickle. The leaves overhead were dusty and hung limp in the thick and humid air. With her fingers she combed her short hair, got the bee settled on her collar again, then set off down the path that led out to the road. A silent Rook took off his long, lordly coat, hung it on a low tree branch, and then followed a few steps behind her. After a short hike, they reached the culvert and climbed up to the gravel road.

Head-high corn stretched to the horizon in rich, green fields, with patches of darker green here and there that were soybean fields. In the misty distance she saw a few farmhouses and outbuildings, and a cloud of dust where a farmer's truck was barreling down another gravel road. Cicadas sounded loud in the air and heat waves shimmered over the corn.

Rook walked beside her rolling up his sleeves, but not saying anything. He probably wasn't feeling all that well, being in the human world like this.

At last they reached the long, rutted driveway leading to Grand-Jane's house.

She got halfway down it before she realized there was something wrong.

Grand-Jane's house was a plain, white box with a front porch and a row of beehives in the side yard. There should've been bees zipping from the nearby lavender field back to the hives, and maybe some sheets hanging out to dry on the clothesline, and a neat herb garden should be growing in the backyard.

But all was silent except for the buzz of the cicadas. Weeds and knee-high grass choked the yard; the windows were blank and closed. A patch of shingles was missing from the roof.

Oh, no. How long had it been?

"It was spring last time I was here," she said aloud. But not the spring before this summer. Maybe the one before that. She'd been gone for over a year. "This much time shouldn't have passed." She led Rook around the side of the house to the kitchen door. Her heart was pounding with worry. She pushed the door open. "Grand-Jane?" she called, though she knew her grandma wasn't in the house.

The kitchen was dark; dust covered every surface. The air felt heavy and hot. A lone housefly buzzed against a dirty windowpane. On the windowsill over the sink, Grand-Jane's pots of herbs were shriveled and brown.

Grand-Jane wasn't . . . she couldn't be . . .

"Here's a letter," Rook said from over by the table. He held it out and she took it, then went outside the stuffy kitchen and into the backyard to read it. It was from a neighbor, a farmer who'd sold them eggs and had sometimes paid Fer to weed his kitchen garden. Fer shook her head; it seemed like such a long time since she'd been that girl living in this house in the middle of the cornfields.

Jennifer,

the letter said.

Your grandmother asked me to come by and leave you a note. She took sick and is living at the Windmill Care Center in town. She said to tell you to come see her if you can.

"Took sick," Fer murmured. And she hadn't been here to help.

Rook was reading over her shoulder. "What's that mean, *care center?*"

Fer shook her head. "It's a nursing home." He wouldn't understand that, either, so she added, "It's a place where old people go to be taken care of if they can't take care of themselves."

"They don't stay with their own people?" Rook asked.

Fer shook her head. It was too hard to explain how things worked in the human world. "I have to go see her."

"Let's go, then," Rook said, and before she could blink, a black horse with a tangled mane and flame-bright eyes was standing on the grass where Rook had been.

Puck, she reminded herself. *Not a friend; not to be trusted.*

Still, she had to get to Grand-Jane. She grabbed his mane and swung onto his back.

Rook raced along the gravel roads, staying to the grass on the side, following her directions as she shouted them. Her bee streaked behind them, buzzing loudly. As they neared town, he slowed down and she slipped to the ground, her bee settled on her collar again, and Rook shifted back to his person shape.

He staggered a bit and then straightened, panting.

She knew where the nursing home was—a three-story

159

building in the center of town, across from the public library. She'd never been inside it.

She and Rook walked along the sidewalks; he was staring around with obvious fascination. It seemed like so long since she'd been here; it was easy to see how strange it must look through his eyes. The asphalt streets, the cracked sidewalks, the dusty windows of the store-fronts, the parked pickup trucks, the barbershop with the striped pole out front, the fire station. A few people were around, but this was a farming town, so most people lived out in the country.

She led Rook up the front steps of the nursing home and inside. She was a few paces down the hall before she realized that he had stopped in the doorway. She turned. "Come on," she whispered.

"It smells wrong," he said.

She sniffed. The air was cool from air-conditioning. He was right, though—it did smell wrong. Like ammonia and floor wax and some kind of medicine that prickled in her nose. "I don't like it either," she said. "You can wait outside if you want to." Not waiting to see what he decided to do, she continued down the hall to an information desk, where a redheaded nurse was talking on a phone.

After a moment, Rook stepped up beside her. He stared at the nurse. "Why is she talking to that thing in her hand?" he whispered.

Another thing too complicated to explain. "Shhh," she whispered back.

The nurse hung up the phone and gave Fer and Rook a long, summing-up look. "How can I help you?" she said, and Fer could hear the doubt in her voice. For a second she saw what the nurse saw: a skinny girl with spiky blond hair and jeans with holes in them and a jacket made of patches with a huge bee buzzing on the collar, and a shaggy-haired, rather dangerous-looking boy with what looked like a black tattoo across his left hand.

Fer took a deep breath and put some Lady-like snap into her voice. "What room is Jane Woods in?"

The nurse raised eyebrows that had been drawn on her forehead in brown pencil. She checked a computer screen. "Two fourteen," she answered. "And what do you want with her?"

"She's my grandmother," Fer answered briskly.

The nurse nodded slowly. "And you are . . . ?"

"I'm her granddaughter," Fer answered. Obviously. "Jennifer."

Rook bumped her arm. "Fer, this isn't going to work," he whispered.

Yes, it was. "I want to see her now, please," Fer said.

"Uh-huh." The nurse narrowed her eyes. "Ms. Woods's granddaughter ran away from home a long time ago. She might have been about your age when she left, but that was years ago." She pointed at a sign on the desk. "Anyway, visiting hours are over. If you want to see Ms. Woods, you'll have to come back tomorrow."

Fer felt a surge of angry impatience. "Fine," she said, and spun on her heel, stalking to the door. The need to see Grand-Jane boiled up in her. She hurried down the sidewalk. The sun was setting, casting orange beams across the sky.

Rook caught up to her on the sidewalk out front. "Fer, I'm not going to be much use to you if we stay here until tomorrow."

"Don't worry," she said shortly. "We won't be staying that long. Come on." She led him to a bench across the street from the nursing home, where she sat down. She was still a little weak from the fever and her legs were shaking, so it felt good to sit, at least for a while. Rook sat on the bench next to her; after a while he pulled up his knees and rested his head on them. The human world was making him feel awful, she knew. He wouldn't be able to eat or drink or sleep until they went back through the Way to the Summerlands, and he probably had a terrible headache on top of that.

She shouldn't be worried about him. He wasn't her friend; he was here by his own choice; he wasn't her responsibility.

When Rook spoke, his voice was muffled; he kept his head down on his knees. "You said too much time has passed here," he said.

She nodded. "I think so. I didn't think I was gone for this long."

"It must be the stilth," he said.

She thought about it. Back when the Mór had stained the Summerlands with the blood of its Lady, the bad things that had happened there had overflowed into the human world.

"Humans are changeable," Rook said. He'd propped his head on his arms to look sideways at her. Her bee had settled on his shoulder, but he didn't seem to notice. "Old Scrawny told me that."

"They are," Fer said. "We are, I mean." Things did move fast in the human world. Humans loved new things; they loved change, progress. Sometimes that was a good thing, she thought, but it could be a bad thing too. She pondered it. The broken oaths of the Forsworn were making the stilth—stopped time—spread through their lands. They might be having an effect here, too— but the opposite effect. If the river of time was flowing faster in the human world than it should be, it was a good thing she'd come when she had. If she'd waited any longer, Grand-Jane might have been swept away, gone forever.

While she thought, the sky grew dark, and a few cars drove past on the street. Rook lifted his head to stare at the headlights as they passed, but didn't ask what they were. Even though the sun had gone down, the air was heavy with heat and humidity.

Fer's head ached just a little from coming into this world. She wouldn't fade like Rook if she stayed here, but after not too long the headache would get worse and she'd get a rash, and everything would start looking grim and gray. Her own land, where she could feel every blade of grass and breeze and leaf in the forest, felt very far away. Her heart longed toward it.

But it longed for Grand-Jane, too.

Finally it was time.

nineteen

It was the middle of the moonless night. The human town was silent and deserted and dark, except for a few magical glowing lights on poles and some other lights in the wrong-smelling building across the road.

"It's time," Fer whispered. "I'm going to try this." She stood and started toward the building.

He jumped up to follow. "I can help," he offered.

She glanced aside at him, then nodded. "Okay. Come on."

He followed her across the road. It was clear enough that Fer was not feeling very friendly toward him. While they'd been sitting on the bench, she'd been rubbing at the place over her heart where the broken end of the thread was probably jabbing at her. She hadn't seemed to realize she was doing it.

He followed Fer around the side of the big building until they found a door propped open with a wedge to let air in. Fer led him through the door to a long hallway with flickering lights that made his headache even worse. His nose twitched. The *care center* smelled strongly strange and wrong, like sickness and something else almost like poison, but not quite. He growled a little, deep in his chest.

"Wait here," Fer whispered, and slipped through another door, leaving him in the cold hallway. He leaned against the wall and closed his eyes. His headache was still eating away at him with nasty, sharp teeth. He waited.

A touch on his shoulder and he flinched and opened his eyes.

"Shhh," Fer whispered. "It's on the second floor." She led them farther down the hallway to some stairs and started up; he followed. She stopped at a landing beside a door. "Okay, Rook," she said. Her eyes looked very large in her pale face. "Since you want to help, I need a distraction. Can you cause some trouble?"

What kind of stupid question was that? "Fer, I'm a puck."

"Does that mean you will?" she asked.

As an answer, he gave her a sharp grin.

She didn't smile back; instead she nodded and

explained what she was going to do and what she needed him to do. "Got it?" she asked.

"I do have it, yes," he answered. All of a sudden he was starting to feel better.

"Good. Let's go."

Fer cracked open the door leading from the stairway to the floor where Grand-Jane's room was; she peered into a dimly lit hallway painted dingy green. A little way down the hall to her left was a more brightly lit desk; she could see two nurses there, and an elevator. The nurses looked alert. If she had to stay in the hallway for too long, they would see her. Open doors and a few abandoned wheelchairs lined the hallway.

A buzzer went off and a nurse came down the hallway. Fer held her breath. The nurse swished past, her shoes squeaking on the shiny floor. After a while the nurse came past again, shaking her head and muttering.

This was going to be tricky.

She put her finger up to her collar and let the bee crawl onto it. "Which one is the right room?" she whispered.

The bee bumbled out through the crack in the door. Keeping low to the ground and near the wall, it flew down the hallway to a door not far from the nurses' station. She might be able to get in there without being seen, but getting out was going to be a lot harder.

Okay. Time to try it. She took a deep breath, waiting until both nurses were looking the other direction, then pushed the door open wider and edged out into the hallway. Like a shadow, Rook followed. *That way*—she nodded toward the nurses' station. He shot her a quick grin and ghosted away.

Fer put her head down and darted across the hall and down two doors to the room the bee had flown into.

No cry of alarm. She let out a breath.

The room was dim, lit only by a light turned low. There were two beds; from the first one came the snores of an old woman, sound asleep. Grand-Jane didn't snore like that. Fer crept farther into the room to the second bed. All she could see was a blanket-covered shape. She edged closer and bumped her knee against a table, and something fell onto the floor with a clatter.

She froze. The snorer in the other bed snorted and snuffled, and after a moment her snores started up again. Fer let out a relieved breath.

In the second bed, she could see a white-haired head; in the dim light, two eyes gleamed.

"Jennifer?" Grand-Jane whispered. "Is it you?"

A sudden upwelling of relief and love and happiness stopped Fer's breath for a moment. She wanted to fling herself into Grand-Jane's arms for a hug. Instead she reached out to take her grandmother's hand. It felt frail and bony.

Fer cocked her head, listening for Rook's distraction. She only had a moment. "Grand-Jane," she whispered. "I'm asking for the third time. Will you come through the Way? Will you come live with me in the Summerlands?" She closed her eyes tightly and clung to her grandma's hand, so afraid that she would say no a third time, because that would be the last time, and Fer would never see her again.

From out in the hallway came a shout.

Fer jumped—had she been discovered?

She heard a scream. "It's a dog!" somebody shouted. Then a series of fierce barks and the sound of running feet.

Just the distraction she needed. "We have to go now, Grand-Jane," she said, getting to her feet.

She heard a papery-sounding laugh. "You brought that puck with you."

"Yes," Fer whispered. "Will you come?"

She heard a rustling of sheets, and the shadowy shape in the bed sat up. "Yes, of course I will," Grand-Jane answered.

Quickly fumbling in the dark, Fer found her grandma's bathrobe and helped her shove her feet into a pair of sneakers, leaving the laces untied. The snoring

in the other bed had stopped. "Jane?" asked a quaver-
ing voice.

Another scream from farther down the hallway.
"There's a *horse* down here!" Then a deeper voice shouted,
"Call security!"

"Come on," Fer said urgently.

She heard her grandma laughing softly as she shuffled toward the door—so slowly. Fer went to steady her.
They paused at the door and peeked out. At the other
end of the hallway, a nurse ran past. She heard more
barking and shouting. Her bee buzzed up and landed on
her collar. Time to go.

She and her grandma shuffled out into the hallway.
The nurses were all looking away, toward the direction of the barking. Hurrying, Fer hustled Grand-Jane
through the door to the stairs.

"Nobody saw," she whispered. Grand-Jane started
quickly down, Fer at her elbow, helping her take each
step. Rook would have to find his own way out.

Outside, the bee hovered over her head as she and
Grand-Jane waited in the shadows where she had first
spotted the side door leading in. At the front of the
building were flashing lights—a police car. Then a long
wail of a siren, and a fire truck pulled up and firefighters
swarmed out, followed by a police officer talking on a
radio.

Rook had made a much bigger distraction than she'd needed. If he didn't hurry it might well get them caught.

Still Rook didn't come.

She took a moment to look over her grandma. Grand-Jane was thin, and hunched where she should be tall, and her hair had turned all white, but her eyes sparkled. Carefully Fer hugged her, and Grand-Jane's arms hugged her back with surprising strength.

"I hated that place," her grandma whispered. "Let's get out of here, Jennifer."

"In a minute." Fer glanced toward the nursing home again. Come *on*, Rook. They might not be friends, but she couldn't leave him here.

Finally the side door slammed open and Rook stumbled out, staggering across the sidewalk to where they waited in the shadows. He tripped and went sprawling on the sidewalk at Fer's feet. "Ow."

She crouched beside him. "Are you okay?" She knew how hard it was for him to shift here in the human world.

He laughed. "I went in a box all the way to the ground." He sat up, blinking. "I think my head is going to fall off."

Fer glanced back toward the door. "Were you seen?"

He climbed dizzily to his feet, still grinning. "They're looking for horses and dogs, not me."

Of course. She stood, taking a deep breath. It was

a long way from town back to the Way. "We'll have to start walking," she said. Maybe they could get there before the sun came up and it got too hot. She wasn't sure Grand-Jane could even walk that far. . . .

"Oh, sure, Fer," Rook answered. He stumbled, bumping into her, and she protected her grandma with one arm and grabbed his shoulder with her other hand, steadying him. "Hello, Jane," he said, still smiling.

To Fer's astonishment, her grandmother smiled back. "Hello, Puck," she said. "Can you turn into a horse and carry us?"

"If you don't mind my head falling off on the way there," Rook mock grumbled.

"Stop fussing," Grand-Jane said.

In response, Rook laughed.

Fer stared. It was almost like . . . *they* were friends. "You don't have to do it," she put in quickly. She didn't want to owe Rook any more favors.

"No, we need to hurry back," he said. His hand went to his pocket; he snatched out his shifter-bone and popped it into his mouth. A blur of shadows, and a tall horse with a tangled mane and flame-bright eyes stood before them on unsteady legs.

"You'll have to help me get up there," Grand-Jane said. Fer laced her fingers together to make a step, and her grandma pulled herself slowly onto the horse's back and sat up, clinging to his mane with shaking hands.

Fer jumped up behind her. She could keep her grandma from falling off while they ran.

Rook gave a snort and they were off. Fer clung to Grand-Jane and to Rook's mane as he raced through the streets, his hooves clattering on the road, the sound echoing off the buildings. Maybe in the morning the people who lived in town would wake up and wonder why they'd dreamed about magic and horses and the rushing of wind.

It was still darkest night when they came to the ravine. Rook slowed and picked his way to the narrow path, then snorted and walked along the streambed instead, until they reached the moon-pool in its quiet clearing.

Fer helped Grand-Jane get down and held her arm as they stepped closer to the moon-pool. Rook shifted back and then stood with his eyes closed as if his head really was about to fall off. Fer saw her grandma reach out to take Rook's hand. He nodded without opening his eyes.

Before opening the Way, Fer turned to look at the ravine, the path leading away to the gravel roads, the farms and cornfields, to Grand-Jane's house at the end of its rutted driveway. This might be the last time she ever came here, to the human world where time flowed so quickly by. "Good-bye," she breathed.

She turned back to the moon-pool. In the darkness

it looked like a well of bottomless shadows. Fer reached out and took her grandma's hand.

"I have always wondered," Grand-Jane whispered, "what this would be like."

"Hold on," Fer said, smiling, and they stepped through the Way.

twenty

She knew Rook wasn't really trustworthy, but when he had told her that the stilth was dangerous and deadly, she had believed him. It was her responsibility too, and she had to figure out how to deal with it.

Until Grand-Jane woke up, Fer needed time to think without anybody interrupting her. Rook had fallen asleep the moment they'd come through the Way from the human world, so she didn't have to worry about him. She looked after her grandma, and before dawn she and Phouka rode deep into the forest where the trees were old and strong and quiet, where nobody would bother her. After a while, she slid off Phouka's back and walked on alone. She hadn't had any breakfast, so her stomach felt hollow. The air was chill and gray. The trees still had leaves, but they'd thinned, and she kicked through drifts of red-brown oak leaves and crumpled, yellow birch leaves and another kind of leaves shaped like little, brown mittens.

The land was descending into the long chill of winter; it was like the moon turning from fat, golden full to an icy crescent. She loved this land with every particle of her being. Every Lord or Lady was connected to their land, just as she was. She couldn't understand why the Forsworn and the other Lords and Ladies felt they had to *rule* their lands and their people, instead of just caring for them. But they did rule. They wore glamories that forced obedience and awe, glamories that turned the wearer as chill as winter moonlight. They didn't want to give up that power. But they would have to, or all the lands would die.

Stepping off the path, Fer rested her forehead against the nubbly bark of an oak tree and closed her eyes. She felt the tree's roots probing into the dirt, spread wide for soaking up water and nutrients. She felt its branches reaching into the sky, its few remaining leaves clinging to the tips of twigs. The first chilly breeze that came along would blow them away. She shivered.

Then she felt something else: just a breath of strangeness in her land. She stilled her breath and concentrated. She was the land's Lady, and she could sense the tiniest beetle gnawing on a rotting log deep in the forest, and she could sense the forest itself, washing like a green tide over low hills and up to steep mountains covered with snow.

She clenched her eyes shut, trying to catch the strange something again.

There. A sort of heavy feeling was seeping into her land from the Way—the Way that should be closed except at sunrise and sunset. The land nearest the Way felt still and silent under that heaviness. The trees drooped ever so slightly; the water in a stream slowed; a flock of sparrows huddled together on a branch.

Her eyes popped open. Was this the stilth? In *her* land?

"Oh, no you don't," she whispered to herself. Then, louder, "Phouka!" she called.

The horse crunched through the leaves to her side. "Back home, if you don't mind," she said, and swung onto his back. "Hurry."

Something was on his ear. He twitched to flick it off and heard a telltale buzz, and the stupid bee landed on the tip of his ear again. Rook was snug and warm, curled up in his dog shape sleeping, and he was not waking up so the bee that wasn't supposed to be talking to him told him something he didn't want to know.

Determined, he kept his eyes closed.

Bzzzrzrzhmmmm, the bee said. *Wake up.*

Not listening.

"Hi, Rook," he heard Fer's voice say.

His eyes popped open. The bee flew past and he made a mock snap at it, and its buzz turned teasing. He climbed to his four paws and then stretched and shook his head and, seeing Fer, felt his betrayer tail start to wag. Quickly he spat out his shifter-tooth and shoved it into his pocket.

She was looking him over. Not frowning, exactly, but as if she was trying to see inside his head to what he was thinking. It made him feel prickly.

"So you're still here," Fer said.

"I am, yes," he answered. They stood at the base of the Lady Tree. Fer's bee had flown up into its branches to join the other bees, who waited there in a swarm. He yawned and rubbed the sleep-sand out of his eyes.

"Hm." She stepped past him and started climbing up to the platform where her little house was.

He started to follow, then stopped with his web-stained hand on the rope ladder that led up the tree. It was just one little sound, Fer's *hm,* but it said a lot. It meant she had changed. When she'd first left the human world to come to these lands, she'd been so stupidly trusting. She'd trusted the Mór, and then later she'd trusted Arenthiel, at least for a little while. And she'd trusted him, too, even when she shouldn't have.

And now that she should trust him, that *hm* meant she didn't trust him at all, curse it.

Fer went into her house, where Grand-Jane was lying asleep in her bed. She started preparing herbs and honey, ignoring Rook as he came in and settled by the door. She still wasn't sure what to think about him. Being in the same room with him made her feel raw, as if her heart had been scraped all over and trampled on. Why was he even *here*? Shouldn't he be with his brothers?

Twig brought in a kettle of hot water and she brewed tea; when it was ready, she woke Grand-Jane and helped her sit up, then sat on the floor as she drank the tea. Letting Grand-Jane sleep would be best, but Fer couldn't wait—she needed to be ready to go out and deal with the stilth as soon as the Way opened at sunset.

"Better?" Fer asked.

"Much better," Grand-Jane answered, and sipped her tea. "Saint-John's-wort and ginseng, I think. Excellent choice," she approved. She looked around the room. "This is very nice."

Fer sat on a carpet woven of silk, with red-and-orange leaves on it that blended together like fire. Hangings of the same color covered the wall. It reminded her of Grand-Jane's warm kitchen back in the human world.

Grand-Jane's eyes sharpened as she caught sight of Rook over by the door. "Good morning, Rook," she said.

He gave her a quick grin in return.

Fer blinked. Her grandma hadn't called him *Robin*, his false name. It was strange that he let her use his real name.

Grand-Jane's sharp gaze shifted to Fer. With a thin hand, she stroked the side of Fer's head. "You've cut off all your hair."

"It kept getting tangled," Fer explained.

Smiling, her grandma shook her head. "I should have thought of that years ago." She studied Fer carefully. "You're worried about something, my girl."

Fer nodded. She hadn't had time to explain it while they'd been in the human world, and her grandma had fallen asleep yesterday as soon as they'd arrived at the Lady Tree. She told about the stilth. "It's because of the broken oaths of the Forsworn, and the glamories," she said. "The stilth has started to spread here, into the Summerlands, too. I have to figure out a way to stop it."

"We have to make the Forsworn take off the glamories," Rook put in. "That's the only way to stop the stilth from spreading."

"Rook, I'm not going to force them," Fer insisted. "You already know that. I have to find another way."

He looked away, then nodded.

"I wish I could do something to help," Grand-Jane said.

"You *can* help," Fer realized. "Grand-Jane, I have to leave to fight the stilth, but you're human. If you stay here, your strength can protect the Summerlands. Will you do that?"

Her grandma gave a brisk nod. "Of course. What shall I do?"

Fer felt an easing of her worry. "Once I've gone, stay at the Way. If any stilth comes through, try to push it back. You should have the power to do that, at least for a little while."

"I will," Grand-Jane said.

Fer stood and gave her grandma one last hug. "Thank you," she whispered.

"You're going into danger again, my girl," Grand-Jane whispered back. "Try to be careful."

She knew she couldn't promise that. "Don't worry." She turned toward the door.

"I'll come too," Rook said, getting to his feet.

She studied him. He *seemed* as if he was trying to help. But she still wasn't sure whether she should trust him or not. Instead of answering, she shrugged and went out.

At the bottom of the Tree, she paused and looked around. The dark-purple fallen leaves of the Lady Tree carpeted the ground; the Tree's branches were silver against the gray sky. The air felt chilly and damp. She leaned against the Tree, focusing on her connection with her land. It felt . . . mostly all right, but the stilth was there in the way the land's turn toward winter had slowed. The air felt stuffy and still.

Rook dropped from the ladder, interrupting her. "Well?" he asked. "What now?"

She straightened and rubbed a tired hand across her eyes. He was a puck, and that meant it was really none of his business. "I don't expect you to help me. In fact, I don't even know what you're doing here."

"I know," he answered. He shoved his hands into his pockets and stood frowning at her. "We need to go talk to my brothers."

"I don't want to talk to them," she shot back.

"You should want to," he said. "They have a plan, something to do with the glamories."

A puck plan? *That* was something she could do without. "No," she said, and started walking.

A bound and he'd caught up to her, his yellow eyes flashing. "Fer," he said, grabbing her arm, "my brothers and I can help."

"Your brothers don't even like me," she said. She jerked her arm out of his grip. "They don't like anyone. Why would they help?"

He shrugged. "Because I'll ask them to."

"Because you'll ask them to," she repeated slowly. "Oh, sure, Rook. You expect me to believe that they'll help me just because you're going to ask them to do it?"

He flared up. "What do you know about it, Fer? You don't know anything about pucks. You think you do, but you don't."

She stepped up, toe-to-toe, and gave him just as much flame as he'd given her. "Then tell me!"

He opened his mouth—to snarl at her, she was sure—but then he blinked and closed it again. "Oh." He paused, as if thinking. Then he backed two slow paces away from her and stood with his head down. After a moment, he looked up. "Fer, what do we pucks seem like to you? I mean, what do you think of us?" He spread his arms, as if presenting himself for her inspection.

And there he was, peering warily at her through the shaggy hair that hung down into flame-colored eyes that were smudged with weariness. The shadow-web tracked darkly across his left hand. She thought back to what she knew of the pucks. She thought about the way other people reacted to them. "You're suspicious," she said slowly. "You don't trust anybody. Nobody trusts you. You lie and betray. You don't want to help anybody; you just want to make trouble."

"We are like that, yes." He was nodding.

"But—" She'd just said awful things about pucks, and he *agreed* with her?

"We have to be that way, Fer," he went on. "You know we're different from the rest of the people in the lands. We can't be ruled, we see too much, we like to make trouble, so all the Lords and Ladies hate us, and fear us, and their people do too. They hunt us. When a baby puck is born to any of their people, they leave it by the nearest Way to die."

What? Fer gasped.

He went on, as if leaving babies to die was an ordinary thing. "Fer, part of being a puck is that we're not bound together by oaths. We're not *friends* with each other. We're brothers. We are . . . we're . . ." He paused and seemed to be watching her very closely. "We *stay true* to each other."

She shook her head. They stayed true? "What do you mean?"

He stepped closer, scuffing through the fallen purple-brown leaves of the Lady Tree. "A puck is always true to his brothers. It's part of who we are. It's how we survive. I trust my brothers without question, and in return, they trust me. If I decide I have to do something, all of my brothers support me. *All* of them," he added fiercely. "*Always.*"

So that was *staying true*. Rook was snarly and annoying, but he was right that she hadn't understood what the pucks truly were. It made her look at him differently. Their friendship was still broken and unfixable, but at least now she could see *why*. Every time he'd bumped up against his friendship with her, he'd stayed true to his brothers. They would always come first. It was part of who he was. Not a human boy. A puck.

And now . . .

He said he wanted to help her.

She shook her head. She just wasn't sure. Her head was telling her not to trust him or his puck-brothers. Her heart ached where the sharp end of the broken thread stabbed her.

"Fer," he said, his voice rough. "It's your way to trust."

That was true. "But I've been too trusting," she said slowly. "I can't— I don't think—" she started.

And then she stopped. Two paces away, Rook stood scowling at her, his yellow eyes fierce, his shoulders hunched as if he was awaiting a blow. He was waiting for her to say no.

A low buzz came from the collar of her patch-jacket. One of her bees had followed her and had landed there and was humming at the edge of her hearing.

Rmmmzmrmmmmmmzm.

She blinked, realizing what it was saying. The bees *liked* Rook. With a little shock, she remembered that when she'd been imprisoned in the tower and she'd sent the bee to her friends, it hadn't gone to Fray and Twig. It had gone to Rook.

Trust him, the bee was telling her.

She shook her head. "Rook, why do you care so much about it? The stilth, I mean. You never cared about anything before, except your brothers."

"I don't know, Fer," he answered. Then his face brightened. "No, I do know. It's because of you. I used to be like what you said. I didn't care about anything except being a puck. But you made me change."

"Oh," she said. Her special human talent again, she realized. To bring change.

"You *can* trust me," Rook insisted. "I do want to help, and my brothers will help too. Can I come?"

Slowly she nodded. She would give him this one last chance. On her collar, the bee gave a happy buzz. She didn't feel like smiling, but something about her answer felt right.

twenty-one

Fer had packed herbs and honey into her knapsack. Rook had told her that some of the people he'd seen were wildling, so she brought all of the herbs she had that were used for healing that particular sickness. She'd talked to Fray and Twig about where she was going and how long she'd be gone, and told them to help Grand-Jane defend the Way. She'd hurried to fetch Phouka from his grazing meadow. She'd summoned the rest of her bees. Then she'd found her bow and quiver of arrows. Herbs, horse, bees, bow. It wasn't much, really, but it felt like she was gathering all her strength around her.

"Is it time?" Rook asked. He'd been pacing around the clearing where the Way would open as soon as the sun set.

"Almost," she answered. Phouka stood strong and steady beside her; his black mane hung long and tangled, and his tail brushed the ground. The bees swarmed over her head, their anxious buzzing like a low growl of thunder. The clouds had thickened and a light rain drizzled down. She ran a hand through her short hair; it came away wet. "Here," she said, handing the heavy knapsack to Rook as he paced past her.

He nodded and slung it over his shoulder.

Waiting by the Way, Fer straightened. The clouds hid the setting sun, but she could feel the slow turn of her land toward night. The Way trembled on the edge of opening. "It's almost time," she said.

Rook stepped up next to her. "I'll take you to my brothers."

"First I want you to take me to see the stilth," she said. "I need to understand what it is so I can figure out how to stop it."

"It'll be dangerous," Rook warned.

"I know." The Way opened. "That doesn't matter now. Come on."

Phouka pranced through. She was about to follow him when she felt the heavy, stuck-in-honey feeling of the stilth flowing through the Way, seeping into her land.

Rook grabbed her hand, pulling her, and they stepped

through the Way, stumbling into the land on the other side of it. Her bees zinged distractedly around the briar-edged clearing. Phouka snorted and shook his head.

"It's stronger than I thought it would be," she said. Part of her wanted to go back and defend her land. But she knew she couldn't abandon the rest of the lands to the stilth.

Rook led her across the Briarlands on a path that led to another Way. They walked single file along a narrow path: first Rook, then Fer, and then Phouka behind her, his hooves clopping loudly on the hardened dirt. The Briarland they passed through felt still and silent. No breeze blew; no birds sang. "Where are all the people who live here?" she asked.

"Hiding, maybe," Rook answered. "Or at the Lake of All Ways. The Lady of this land fears the stilth, so she abandoned her land and its people and went into hiding at the nathe."

A Lady abandoning her land and people. Fer shivered at the thought.

Finally they reached the Briarland's other Way and passed through it, stepping into a forested land she'd visited a couple of times. Before, it had been full of trees with fan-shaped leaves, and here and there a meadow bursting with wildflowers and butterflies dancing in the sunlight.

But now all was still, the air heavily silent. Looking around, she saw that thousands of caterpillars had covered the forest with their woven cocoons. The swathes of foglike web made the trees look like ghosts.

Rook went over to one of the trees and reached into a sticky web. He came back to where Fer and Phouka waited. "Look," he said. In his hand he held a brown cocoon. Phouka poked his nose over Fer's shoulder to see it. Carefully Rook started to split it open.

"No—" Fer started. He'd kill the butterfly if he broke its cocoon.

But then she smelled something rotten. Rook picked apart the cocoon to show her what was inside. A slimy lump of a misshapen thing, half butterfly, half caterpillar. Dead.

She looked up at the web-shrouded trees. The butterflies were waiting, waiting, waiting for a change that would never come. They were rotting and dead. "So this is the stilth," she said softly.

"It is, yes," Rook answered. "But there's worse."

"Show me," she ordered. "I need to see it."

Fer let him lead her and Phouka and the bees through another Way, and then another. They passed groups of people, refugees with packs on their backs, headed for the nathe. In their frightened eyes she could see fever— they were wildling, all of them. Finally they came to another Way.

Rook paused and shot her a worried glance. "This is the worst of it, Fer."

"All right." Fer got ready to step through the latest Way.

"They'd better stay here," Rook said, pointing at the swarm of bees hovering over her head. "And you, too, Finn," he said to Phouka.

Staying alert, she left her bees and Phouka and followed Rook through the Way.

They stepped out of it onto a rock ledge overlooking a plain of mud and rot. A virulently red sun burned a hole in the horizon. The sky overhead was soot black, with no stars, no moon. A stench of death washed over her; she choked for breath. Beside her, Rook stood without moving.

"Rook?" she asked, but her words made no sound in the stuffy air.

She turned—slowly, so slowly—and rested a hand on his arm.

At her touch, he gasped, then choked in another breath. He said something that she couldn't hear.

She kept her grip on his arm. His head lifted; the flames in his eyes, she noticed, were dim, like a banked fire.

They had to get out of this dying land. Gripping his hand, she turned them both around and faced the Way. With an arm that felt as heavy as stone, she opened it, then dragged him through.

They stood coughing and gasping for breath on the other side. Phouka stood with stiff legs, snorting, as if he was worried. The bees circled Rook's head, then settled over Fer, buzzing with alarm.

"The Sealands," Rook said, once he could talk again. He glanced over his shoulder at the closed Way they'd just passed through. "It's worse than I thought it would be."

"It's death," Fer realized, and shivered with the horror of it. The stilth was powerful and inevitable. As it spread it would bring its unchanging stillness and silence to all the lands and all of the people who lived in them. What could she possibly do to stop it?

But Rook was standing with his hands on his hips, grinning at her.

"What?" she asked.

"Did you see what happened there, in the Sealands?" he asked. "I was stuck, but you freed me. You have power against the stilth. Old Scrawny said you did because you're part human, and changeable, and he was right."

Yes, she knew she had power, but it didn't seem like much. Not compared to the hugeness and the horror of the stilth.

twenty-two

Rook knew he should have gone back to his brothers before this. They'd be impatient at having to wait so long. They'd want to carry out their puck-plan right away. He didn't know what that plan was, exactly, except that it was supposed to turn everything upside down and had something to do with the shadow-spinner spider. His brothers didn't know about the stilth, and even if they did, they wouldn't care about it because they wouldn't see how it might affect them. Somehow he had to convince them to change their plan—to work with him, and with Fer.

It was like being pulled into pieces, this trying to stay true to Fer and to his brothers at the same time. Pretty soon there wouldn't be anything of himself left at all.

He led Fer and Phouka and the bees through the Way and into the land of the tree-giants. As before, the ground was covered with soft pine needles. The trees towered all around, blocking the sunlight. Rook walked past a root as tall as he was. It made him feel tiny.

As they walked, pine needles from the trees drifted down around them. One landed on Rook's shirtsleeve. It was green on one side, silver on the other, and surprisingly delicate coming from such a huge tree. The needles fell, gleaming as they tumbled through the faint light. They made a sound as they landed, like *tick-tick-tick*.

He stopped. The pine needles were falling as hard as rain.

Fer stepped up next to him. "What?" she asked, her voice quiet in the stuffy air.

This wasn't right. He held up his hand, and a few needles dropped onto it. "The stilth has come here, too," he told her.

A sudden, unexpected, unpucklike knot of worry clenched inside him. The stilth really was spreading, and it was spreading fast—way faster than he'd thought it would. He and Fer might not have much time before all the lands started falling into stillness and death.

He led Fer and the bees and Phouka through the huge trees to the biggest tree of all of them, with the cave dug out of it. His brothers were there, some of them sitting around the campfire, others curled asleep in their dog shapes. He frowned. They were too quiet for pucks.

As they got closer, Asher, Tatter, and Rip came to meet them. They didn't bound this time, or shout out his name as they usually did.

Rook stopped and studied them. Asher's braided hair looked dull; Tatter didn't smile; Rip didn't growl at seeing Fer, and the flame in his eyes looked dim.

The stilth was affecting them, clear enough. "Brothers," he said.

"Rook," Asher replied; then he nodded at Phouka. "Brother," he said to the horse. He looked at Fer, and his eyes narrowed.

Rip grabbed Rook's shoulders with two black-painted hands. "Pup," Rip growled down at him. "We've been waiting for you." He lowered his voice. "Why'd you bring that Lady with you?" He let Rook go and stepped back.

Fer looked fiercely up at the taller pucks. "Hi, Robin," she said to Ash. "Hi, other Robin," she said to Rip, who bared his teeth at her. Then she smiled at Tatter, who nodded back. She rested the end of her bow on the ground and gripped its top. She looked strong and determined. "I assume you know about the stilth," she said to them.

"We do, yes," Ash said warily. "We don't see what it has to do with us."

"Then you're being stupid," Fer said sharply. The bees hovered over her head, grumbling. "When the stilth invades the lands, everyone will die."

"Then go and deal with the stilth, Lady, and leave us out of it," Rip said, putting a bitter accent on the word *Lady*.

Fer glanced aside at Rook. "I thought you said they would help."

He shrugged. "They will." He hoped they would, anyway.

She rolled her eyes. "They don't seem very helpful."

"That's because we're *not* helpful," Ash growled.

Right, time for him to step in. "Fer, this is my brother Asher." Then he pointed at Rip. "And this is Rip. You already know Tatter."

"Brother," Ash growled. He didn't like Rook telling Fer their real names.

Rook ignored him. "They'd be thinking more clearly, Fer, but the stilth has come here." He gave Asher a long look. "You can feel it, can't you?"

After a slow moment, Asher nodded. "We can, yes." Then he shrugged. "We're pucks. We don't have to stay in one land. We'll go somewhere the stilth hasn't come to."

"There's no such place," Rook said. "I've been traveling to as many of the lands that I could get to. The stilth is in the Ways and it's spreading everywhere, even the human world."

"We have to stop it," Fer said. "Rook said you have a plan."

"It's a puck-plan," Rip said, with an edge of his old surliness. "It's for making trouble. It's nothing to do with this stilth of yours."

"He *said*," Fer said firmly, "that you would help."

"They will, Fer," Rook put in. "I just have to talk to them."

"You'll have to talk fast, Pup," Rip growled.

Fer blew out an impatient-sounding breath. "Okay. Sure. Talk to your brothers, Rook." She pointed at the biggest tree. "I'll just go look at that cave over there." Giving all four of them a glare, she stalked off.

Ash, Tatter, and Rip closed in around him.

"We don't like that girl," Rip said grimly.

"You broke the thread," Ash added, "but it's clear, Pup, that she's still got some kind of hold on you."

"A binding spell," Rip put in.

"No, I told you before," Rook said. "That's not it. I—" Curse it. This was where everything could go wrong. "I didn't break the thread. She did. I wanted to be friends with her." He took a deep breath. "Now I want to stay true to her."

"*Stay true?*" Asher asked, his eyes wide.

"She's not a puck," Rip said flatly. "You can't."

Rook's fierceness flared. "I can," he shot back.

Ash shook his head. "You know what that would mean."

"I know, yes," Rook said.

All three of his brothers stared at him for a long, tense moment. The pine needles floated down around them.

"You'd ask that of us?" Ash said softly.

"I do ask it," Rook answered.

His brothers were silent. He knew how hard this was for them to understand, him staying true to Fer. The pucks were separate, alone. A puck never helped anyone but another puck. A puck never stayed true to anyone but another puck.

He'd been like that, once. He was still a puck, but because of Fer—because of strange, stubborn, loyal, part-human Fer—he'd been changed. He'd learned how to care about other people. He'd found he could have friends who weren't pucks, who knew his real name and called him by it. He'd realized that when there was something wrong, like the stilth, he could help to set it right.

His brothers couldn't understand any of that. They had their plan, and they couldn't see beyond it.

Ash glanced aside at Tatter and shrugged. "He's always been a strange one, hasn't he?"

Tatter nodded. "He has, yes."

"Always out and about," Ash said.

"A wanderer," Rip confirmed.

The three of them stood looking at him; he waited warily to see what they would decide.

Then Asher stepped closer and slung an arm over Rook's shoulders. "Brother," he said.

Rip gripped Rook's arm. "Brother," he added, with a sharp grin.

Tatter leaned in and kissed the side of Rook's head, then ruffled his hair. "Brother."

Rook let out a shaky, relieved breath. No matter what strange thing they thought he was up to, they would always stay true to him, and he would stay true to them.

That's what it meant to be a puck.

twenty-three

Before the pucks told her and Rook their plan, they decided they needed to have supper. Fer told them she was a vegetarian, and after she had explained that *vegetarian* meant she didn't eat meat, and the pucks had laughed with disbelief at that, one of them found a potato and put it in the coals of their campfire to cook; another brought out an apple he'd stolen from somewhere and gave it to her.

They settled down to eat. Night had fallen and the air grew cooler, and Fer sat close to the campfire to stay warm. Sparks from the fire floated into the darkness and winked out. Her bees darted among the sparks, as if playing a game with them. The pucks roasted rabbit and squirrel meat over the flames. With gleaming eyes they watched Fer dig the potato out of the fire with a stick. Then they watched her eat it.

"Surely you've seen somebody eat a vegetable before," she muttered, and they laughed.

Even without salt or butter, the potato was hot and good, the skin charred from the coals. She saw Rook eat a rabbit leg and toss the bones over his shoulder. Phouka stood behind her, munching on a pile of hay one of the other pucks had brought him.

Strangely, even while worry about her own land gnawed at her, and while she knew the stilth was continuing its relentless spread, she felt happy. She actually *liked* the pucks, especially seeing them all together like this. The baby, Scrap, was toddling around the circle, getting a kiss or a hug from each of his brothers before being sent on. They teased and laughed, and—she could see it clearly—they loved one another. In everything they did, they *stayed true*, just like Rook had told her they did.

Across the campfire, Rook tossed a last bone over his shoulder; then he wiped his face on his sleeve and grinned at her. "Okay, Fer," he said. "Now Ash is going to tell us the plan."

The puck Asher stood. The crystals woven into his long braids glinted in the firelight. "Lady," he said, with a nod to Fer. "You know enough about us pucks to know that we can see through lies, and we don't like the glamories."

Yes, she knew that. She nodded.

Asher went on. "We figure that if the Lords and Ladies—all of them, not just the Forsworn—have their glamories stripped away, their people will see what they truly are, and they won't be able to rule anymore. It'll turn everything upside down."

Fer frowned. *Stripping the glamories.* It sounded like what Rook had done to the Birch-Lady with his web-stained hand. Which had been horrible and wrong.

"Tell her how," Rip growled. In his black-painted face, his orange eyes glittered.

Asher gave a sharp-toothed grin. "Our Pup has told you about the shadow-spinner spider, hasn't he?"

She gave a slow nod—yes.

"We're going to kidnap the Lords and Ladies, starting with the Forsworn," Asher said. "Then we'll take them to the spider's chasm and throw them in."

"It's brilliant!" shouted one of the pucks. A few other pucks laughed.

Fer shook her head. The weight of worry piled onto her shoulders again. "No," she said firmly.

The pucks stopped laughing. "What did you say?" Rip asked, his voice low and dangerous.

"You can't force them like that," Fer answered.

"We can, yes," Asher said. He strode around the fire to loom over her like a storm cloud, his flame-colored eyes flashing. "They chose to rule. That means they have no choice about this."

Fer stood and faced him down. "They *have* to choose, pucks!" She cast a glance at Rook. "You saw what happened with the Birch-Lady, Rook. We could have killed her, destroying her glamorie the way we did. They are our enemies, but even so, we can't risk killing the Forsworn."

Rook shook his head. "The Birch-Lady was bad, Fer, but the stilth is worse. My brothers are right. We have to do it this way."

"This is our plan, Lady," Rip snarled. "Take it or leave it."

Pucks! She clenched her fists, ready to argue it out with them, except . . .

Except they *were* right, sort of. The Lords and Ladies and the Forsworn were *not* going to choose to change—she knew that. They were stuck in their glamories, just like flies stuck in a spiderweb. She remembered the second time she'd worn a glamorie—taking it off had been *so* hard. It had set into her skin and bones as if it were made of fishhooks. Ripping it off had *hurt*. It had been the hardest thing she'd ever done, and she'd only been wearing the glamorie for a day.

"Come *on*, Fer," Rook said, interrupting her thoughts.

"Wait," she said, holding up a hand as the new thought came to her. "I know the Forsworn are causing the stilth," she said. "But what if they want to change and can't?" The pucks stared at her with gleaming eyes, and she went on. "They've been wearing the glamories for maybe hundreds of years. Taking them off might be impossible for them."

"It doesn't matter anymore," Rook said. "It's too late."

Rip gave her a sullen stare, and Ash shook his head. "We need to use the spider," he said.

"Ooookay," she said, thinking. "I agree with that part of it. What if . . ." She smiled. The pucks were going to love this idea. "The nathe is the center of everything. It's where the Lake of All Ways is, and it's where the Forsworn have gathered, and so have all the other Lords and Ladies. If we want to stop the stilth, it has to be from there. What if we go and get the spider and bring it with us to spin its webs at the nathe?"

Ash gave her a narrow-eyed glance. "And then what, Lady?"

She went on, thinking it through. "We have to give them one more chance to choose. *All* of the Lords and Ladies, not just the Forsworn ones." She shot Asher a quick grin. "It'd turn things upside down, wouldn't it, if they did?"

He barked out a laugh. "It would, yes!"

But Rip still looked fierce and grim. "I like the part about trapping the spider and bringing it to the nathe," he put in. "But we know the Lords and Ladies. They are not going to take off their glamories unless we force them to do it. Especially these Forsworn ones." He glared around the fire at the other pucks. "You know I'm right, brothers."

Fer couldn't argue with that. If Rip was right and the Forsworn refused to take off their glamories, it would mean death for everyone in all the lands. She would try as hard as she could to convince the Forsworn to fulfill their oaths, but if she couldn't, she and the pucks wouldn't have any choice. It wouldn't be a good choice, but it'd be the only one left to them. "Okay," she said.

The pucks stared at her. "What?" Asher asked.

"*Okay* means *all right*," Rook explained.

"Good!" Ash shouted.

The other pucks got to their feet and crowded around her, talking and jostling and laughing. She stumbled as one puck tousled her short hair and another gave her an approving slap on the shoulder. For the first time in a long time she felt light and free and wild, not a Lady with terrible responsibilities, but a kid laughing with her friends. They grinned at her and she grinned back at them, and for just a moment she felt accepted—part of their pack, one of the pucks.

twenty-four

Night fell. Rook and his brothers hurried to get ready. All the pucks had something to carry. Six pucks together had the huge net that they'd woven from sturdy rope to imprison the captured Lords and Ladies in; now they'd use it to trap the spider. They strapped the net to two long poles that they hoisted onto their shoulders. Some had spears they'd stolen from various guards and fighters in other lands. Phouka had packs full of food slung over his back. Rook had a coil of rope over one shoulder and a bundle of firewood over the other, and he'd exchanged his lordly, silk shirt for a plain, gray shirt like the ones his brothers wore. Fer, he saw, had turned her patchwork jacket inside out; its lining was brown, and she blended with the night, except for her lighter shock of hair.

As the full moon rose behind a veil of clouds, the ten pucks chosen to carry out the plan, plus Fer and Phouka, tramped through the land of the tree-giants, and out the Way. In the lands there were hundreds of Ways, and pucks knew all the shortcuts and all the secret, little-used Ways, and soon they were standing in a quiet crowd before the Way that opened only at midnight.

It felt good to be with his brothers; he'd been away from them too much lately. Rook was glad Fer had agreed to come too. It made him feel less pulled into pieces to have her here with them.

"It's an excellent plan, isn't it?" Ash said, and Rook saw a flash of Fer's teeth as she grinned.

"The plan is terrifying," Rook said, and then he laughed. Capturing the muck-spider. A perfectly puck-like plan—and it had been all Fer's idea.

"You're doing it again, dear Pup," Tatter whispered from beside him.

What?

His brother reached out and touched him on the chest, and Rook realized that he was rubbing the spot over his heart where the broken thread was. Quickly he shoved his hand into his pocket.

"It's time," Ash said with a glance at the sky. "You're ready?"

"I am, yes," Rook answered.

"And you, Lady?" he asked.

"Ready," Fer said firmly.

They stepped into the Way that led to the land of the spinners.

𝄢 𝄢 𝄢

The moon, a little off full, spilled milky light over the smooth, black stone of the Spinnerlands. Fer kept up with the ten pucks as they trotted, and with Phouka, whose hooves clattered over the rock. She had her bow and quiver full of arrows, and they bumped on her shoulder as she ran. Rook pointed out to her the spire where the moon-spinner spider had woven its glamorie webs. As they passed it, she looked for the spider, but it was nowhere to be seen. Maybe it really was dead. Leaving the spire behind, they hiked way out over the rock plain until they reached a wide hole in the ground that was so dark it sucked the moonlight into itself.

"That's it," Rook whispered. The chasm where, he'd told her, the shadow-spinner spider lurked in its stench and muck.

The Way out of this place wouldn't open again until midnight tomorrow, so the pucks set up camp at the edge of the chasm. They'd wait until tomorrow night to carry out the plan. Fer tried to ignore the nagging worry she felt about the spreading of the stilth, and used the rest of the night and a good part of the next day to catch up on her sleep. Then, as Rook and his brothers practiced with the net and with their stolen spears, she set up a target and took some shots with her bow and arrows.

Finally night came on again and Asher called them all to the edge of the chasm. Fer gathered her bees and told them to wait with Phouka, and then wedged herself into the huddle. The pucks around her were dark shadows with flame-bright eyes. "We've got to have the spider captured and back to the Way by midnight," Ash whispered. "Rook's been down there before. What can you tell them, Pup?"

Rook crouched, and on the moonlit rock he traced the layout of the chasm. "The path, here," he pointed, "goes down to a ledge that isn't very sturdy." He looked up at her and his brothers. "The spider's got babies, too," he added. "Lots of them, all about this big." He held up his hand to show them.

"Careful of the babies, then," Tatter murmured. All the pucks nodded at that.

Fer blinked, surprised. She wouldn't have expected that kind of care from the pucks.

"I know the way down," Rook whispered. "I'll go first, if you like."

Fer's stomach lurched. To go first was the most dangerous. She wanted to warn Rook to be careful, but she knew that wouldn't be a pucklike thing to do, so she kept quiet.

"Very good, Pup," Ash said.

As Rook stood, Rip handed him a spear. Then Rip turned and offered Fer a spear of her own. "This is a sharp one, Lady," he said. For the plan, Rip had painted himself all black; he looked like a puck-shaped hole in the night, with two spots of flame for his eyes.

"It's okay," Fer said, lifting her bow, and shrugging her shoulder to show him that she was carrying her quiver of arrows. "All right, I mean. I have these."

Rip grinned, and his teeth didn't flash white in the moonlight; he'd painted them black too.

Asher handed around scraps of cloth—so the stench wouldn't overwhelm them, he said—and they all tied them over their noses and mouths.

"Ready?" Asher asked, his voice muffled by the cloth. Fer nodded.

"Ready," Rook answered.

"Good." Asher patted him on the shoulder. "Let's catch ourselves a muck-spider."

Gripping her bow, Fer followed Rook and his brothers into the chasm.

Rook lay on the narrow ledge overlooking the bottom of the chasm, where the shadow-spinner spider squatted in its swamp of muck. The stench was as bad as ever; he was glad for the cloth covering his mouth and nose.

He and his brothers and Fer had made their attempt

on the spider the previous night. They'd gone in with their spears and their net, and the spider had come at them with the sharp pincers at the end of its fore-legs, and its babies had darted out and bit three pucks with their needle fangs. By the time he and Fer and the rest of the pucks had dragged themselves out of the chasm, defeated, it was too late to get through the Way. They'd spent all day mending the damaged net, and Fer and Tatter had worked to heal his three spider-bitten brothers.

Tonight they would try again. Just the seven of them, this time, and Fer, while the three bitten ones rested on the rock above.

Rook gripped his spear and peered into the dark-ness. His ribs hurt, bruised where one of the spider's long legs had flailed last night and hit him. His fine boots and trousers were filthy with muck, and his gray shirt was torn. His brothers and Fer were no better off, but they were determined to succeed tonight. They had to. The longer they stayed here, the farther the stilth would spread.

A layer of ragged clouds covered the moon, so no light shone into the chasm. That might make better hunting for them, Rook figured. If they were quiet enough, the spider might not hear them coming.

Fer dropped silently to the ledge, then lay down beside

him. She had her bow in her hands. "See anything?" she whispered.

No. But he could *feel* it. And smell it.

Last night they'd tried to drop the net down from above. The spider had slashed it with its pincers and driven Fer and the pucks back. Tonight they'd have to try something else.

Rook pushed down the cloth covering his mouth so Fer would hear him. "I think we've got to get the net under it," he whispered.

"Draw it off first, you mean?" she asked.

"I do, yes." Rook rubbed the back of his hand across his eyes, which burned from the stench of the muck. "It might as well be me that does it." He pointed with his chin toward the bottom of the chasm, which was dank with shadows. "It's waiting. I'll go down and lure it away."

One of his brothers dropped onto the ledge beside them. "And we lay out the net and lure it back, is that it?" Asher asked.

"That's it, Brother," Rook answered.

"I'm coming with you, Rook," Fer whispered.

He glanced aside at her and nodded. Her blond hair was clotted with mud, and her face was smudged, and she had a bruise on her chin. She'd been as brave as any puck the night before; it'd be good to have her with him tonight. "Once you've lured it onto the net," he told Ash, "be ready to pull it up quick." If they didn't, he and Fer would be trapped on the other side of the chasm and the spider would get them for sure.

"Not to worry, Pup." It was too dark to see, but Rook could hear the grin in Asher's voice. "We'll shift to horses up there and tie on the ropes, and we've got Phouka to help too. We'll have the spider out in no time."

When his brothers had the net ready, Rook slipped from the ledge, then half climbed, half fell to the bottom of the chasm. He heard a glooping sound as Fer landed beside him, and then a gasp as the stench hit her. Muck and mud and shadow-spun web clung to his boots; he gripped his spear to balance. His eyes watered from the horrible smell. He blinked and peered into the shadows.

Lots of tiny, gleaming eyes peered back. He nudged Fer and pointed. She nodded, seeing them.

"Hellooooo, babies," he breathed.

Moving as stealthily as he could, using his spear as a staff, he led Fer along the edge of the chasm. His boots were heavy with muck. The tiny eyes watched. In the shadows beyond them, the big spider moved. He heard the sucking of the mud as it shifted.

"Do you hear it?" he whispered.

"It's following us," Fer whispered back.

Good. The spider had to follow them to give his brothers room to lower the net. He kept going, leading Fer over muck-smeared rocks, ducking under rags of clotted shadow-web. The spider lurched after them.

At last they made it to the other side of the chasm. The clouds over the moon had thinned; it was light enough that he could see the bulk of the muck-spinner spider looming closer. A long, pincer-tipped leg probed out from the shadows.

He and Fer cringed away from it.

"Any time would be good, brothers," he muttered to himself. They had to have the net ready by now; they needed to draw the spider away from him and Fer.

The clouds thinned even more. A slurp of mud, and the spider eased closer. Its horse-sized body was coated with muck and bristling with sharp spikes. Its jointed legs clicked like bones as it moved. Its stench wafted around him. Rook couldn't see its eyes, but he could feel it . . . sizing him up.

Pucks were *not* food. "Brothers!" he yelled.

At the sound of his voice, the spider struck out toward Rook with a long, many-jointed, muck-dripping leg. The blow slammed him against the rock wall; the spear slipped from his grasp.

"No!" he heard Fer shout, and an arrow whanged off the spider's armored back.

The spider drew back its leg again, ready for a killing strike.

Rook flinched away, holding up his left hand to block the blow.

Which didn't come.

The pincer hung before his face. A stray beam of moonlight glittered along its razor-edge. Rook held his breath. The pincer turned; it came closer. The spider loomed up before him like a spiky wall. Then Rook felt the sharp tip of the pincer touch his hand. It traced the shadow-web that was stuck to his palm.

Rook held himself still and tried not to breathe. What was it *doing*?

"Rook, get down," Fer shouted. He caught a quick glimpse of her, five paces away, as she stood braced, drawing another arrow from her quiver. She'd put the arrow in the spider's eye this time, Rook knew.

"Wait," he gasped. "Fer, don't shoot."

The giant spider squatted in the mud, glistening in the moonlight. It was a lot bigger than he'd first thought. It was bigger than a horse. It was bigger than *two* horses. It had that many legs, anyway. Its huge, bulbous, brown-and-black body was suspended between spiked and jointed legs, with a smaller front section where its two glossy, black eyes seemed fixed on him. On either side of its mouthparts were two shorter feelers covered with spiky fur just like its legs.

"Hellooooo, spider," Rook breathed, keeping his web-stained hand raised.

The spider eased even closer. With its short feelers, it tapped Rook's hand. Then it patted him all over while its glittering eyes examined him. Its mouthparts clicked and gurgled, and Rook felt a jolt of fright—*pucks are not food!*—and then the spider started growling.

He stumbled back until he was pressed against the stone wall of the chasm. The spider lurched forward and stood over him, still growling. He looked up to see its looming body, its legs arching over him. The growl grew louder, like a low roll of thunder.

"Rook . . ." he heard Fer say. "I'm still not-shooting here."

"It's okay," he said, Fer's human word. Slowly he edged away from the spider, along the wall.

"Rook, it's *growling* at you," she said fiercely, keeping an arrow trained on the spider.

"Not growling," he told her. It was . . . it sounded like it was *purring*. With a front leg, the spider reached out to touch him, and knocked him against the wall again.

Then, from the other side of the chasm came a shout that echoed from the rocky walls. The spider jerked its leg away, then lurched toward the sound. It dragged itself through the mud. Rook heard a thrashing sound, more shouts, and then a yell of triumph.

His brothers had caught it, then.

Rook let out his breath and leaned against the wall, his legs shaking. His entire right side ached as if it was one giant bruise.

Fer came to lean on the wall next to him. "What just happened, Rook?"

He gave a half laugh and shook his head. The spider hadn't killed him when it could have, easily. He looked down at his web-smudged hand, which the spider had examined so carefully.

"Come on," Fer said. "We need to get out of here."

With Fer at his side, he limped across the muddy swamp of the chasm floor, watched by the many shining eyes of the baby spiders. "You can come out if you want," he told them, not really thinking they'd understand.

He and Fer helped each other climb up to the ledge. From above, he heard more shouts, then a whinny from Phouka. Wearily he followed Fer up the path. At the top he dragged himself out of the chasm and lay flat on the rock.

About twenty paces away, the setting moon shone down on the huge, shadowy bulk of the spider, wrapped in the net so tightly that its legs couldn't get loose to slice the ropes. His brothers were busy tying the net down, scraping the muck off, laughing. They all had bits of shadow-web stuck to themselves; one puck had it splashed across his face and was proudly showing it to his envying brothers. One puck shifted into his dog shape and lifted his muzzle to howl joyfully at the setting moon.

"We've done it, then," Fer said.

"We have, yes," Rook answered, and closed his eyes.

twenty-five

"Getting that thing through the Way is going to be a trick, don't you think, Lady?" Asher asked. He pointed at the spider in its net. It thrashed against the thick ropes, stilled, and then thrashed again.

She nodded. Not just getting it through the Way, but getting it to spin its web at the nathe without actually killing anybody. Though the pucks might not care about that, as long as it wasn't a puck who was killed. She frowned and nudged a cup of the tea she'd made closer to the fire, keeping it warm until Rook woke up. Then she took a sip from her own cup. The other pucks were there, Tatter and Phouka, too, some of them sleeping, some mending holes in their clothes, some drinking the healing tea she'd made.

She glanced aside to check on Rook and saw that he'd opened his eyes.

"The spider's not dead, is it?" he croaked.

"It's not, no," Ash answered. Then he gave a gleeful grin. "Just biding its time, I think." At that, the other pucks around the fire laughed. "It'll bide until the Way opens tonight."

Moving slowly, as if he hurt all over, Rook sat up.

Fer handed him the cup of tea. "Here. It'll make you feel better."

"Thanks," he said, and rubbed his eyes.

Rip came up then. "Look at what I've got," he said with a sharp grin, holding up his arm to show them. Clinging to his wrist was a fat, needle-fanged baby spider.

"Brother!" Asher said, jumping to his feet. Tatter scrambled away. Phouka gave a nervous whinny.

"No, look," Rip said. He held up a web-smudged finger. Instead of biting it, the baby rubbed a foreleg against it. Rip opened his hand, and the spider crawled onto it; he lifted the spider to his ear, listening. "It's purring," he said. "It likes me."

Asher laughed. "It does like you!"

Rook had put down his cup of tea and was climbing creakily to his feet. "We might as well see if this works," he said, starting toward the huge, net-wrapped spider.

Fer jumped up and rushed to his side. "Rook, what are you doing?"

He shot her a sharp, sideways grin. "The baby spider is purring, my brother said."

"Yes, purring," Fer said as they reached the huge spider. "So?"

"It's because he's got a bit of web on him, I think," he explained, and raised his own web-smudged hand. "Just like this."

The other pucks had gathered behind them. "What're you thinking, Pup?" Ash asked.

Rook nodded at the huge spider. It strained against the thick ropes of the net. Then it stilled. Fer could see one of its multifaceted, black eyes watching them.

"This might be the stupidest thing I've ever done," Rook muttered.

Fer bet he had done some extremely stupid things in his life so far too.

"Set it loose," he ordered.

Fer expected his brothers to protest, but three of them jumped to the ropes that were holding down the net and untied them; then they pulled the heavy net off the spider.

Slowly, stiffly the spider unfolded itself and then flipped onto its pincer-tipped legs. Fer gulped. It loomed, bulbous and huge, twice as tall as any of the pucks.

"Helloooo, spider," she heard Rook whisper as he held up his web-smudged hand.

The spider gave its deep growl, and then it leaped on Rook, knocking him to the ground.

The pucks scattered, and Fer yelped and then turned to run back to the fire, where she'd left her bow and arrows.

Tatter grabbed her arm. "Wait."

The pucks were edging closer to the spider. "You all right, Pup?" Ash asked, bending to peer under the spider's huge bulk.

"I am, yes," she heard Rook's rough voice answer. He crawled out from under the spider and got to his feet. The spider's hairy front feelers tapped him all over, as if checking to be sure he wasn't hurt. He pushed the spider's feeler away and grinned. "It's tamed to me, brothers," he said. He pointed at the much smaller spider clinging to Rip's arm. "Just as Rip's baby, there, is tamed to him. Like a pet!"

The spider growled its rumbling purr, and one of the feelers stroked Rook's head hard enough that he stumbled.

Asher caught his arm and steadied him. Then he laughed. "Are you sure the spider is your pet, Pup, and not the other way around?"

Rip and Tatter laughed, and Fer couldn't help but

laugh too. Rip's baby spider was waving its front legs. Maybe that was how spiders laughed.

"Oh, sure," Rook grumbled, and shoved the spider's feeler off the top of his head.

"I want a pet spider too," Tatter said.

"We should all have pet spiders!" Asher exclaimed.

Laughing, the pucks, including Phouka, dashed toward the chasm, determined to get pet spider-babies of their own.

Fer was left facing Rook. "Well," she said, and she couldn't help the laugh that was bubbling up inside her. They were all in terrible danger from the stilth, and time might be running out, but the pucks were sure a lot of fun.

As the afternoon ended and night came on, the pucks swirled around Fer, getting ready to go as soon as the Way opened. She found her bow and quiver and slung them over her shoulder, and made sure Rook had her knapsack full of healing herbs and tinctures. Phouka pranced and showed off the baby spider perched between his pricked ears. Her bees hovered overhead.

"We can go straight there," Asher said, coming up to her.

Some of the pucks had shifted into their dog forms; others were horses; some stayed in their person shapes.

They crowded around her, ready to leave. Rook stood a little apart from them with the huge spider looming behind him.

Fer nodded at Asher and turned to face them. "Listen, you pucks," she said loudly, and after a few jeers and laughs, they quieted. "I'm not sure what we'll find at the Lake of All Ways." She gripped her bow. "We know the Forsworn have been gathering power, and it's possible they'll be waiting for us, prepared to attack, so be ready." They'd kidnapped her once; they might be planning something new. "Or we might just find a lot of people who are wildling and afraid." She gave them a hard look. "They'll be afraid of you, too, pucks, and Rook's spider, so try to be nice to them."

More jeers and laughter. She rolled her eyes. Pucks!

She led them over the plain of rock to the Way. "Are you ready?" she asked as midnight approached.

Sudden dark seriousness. "We are, yes," Rook answered for all of them.

"Let's go," she said, and stepped into the Way.

twenty-six

Passing through the Way from the land of the spiders to the Lake of All Ways was like trying to walk against the flow of a river in full flood. The stilth lurked in the Ways, gathering its strength, and it pushed against her, trying to force her back. Fer gritted her teeth, and to get them all through it drew on the same stubborn spark of human-ness that had gotten her out of the time-spelled tower.

To her surprise, as that spark flared, the stilth pulled away. At first going through was as hard as climbing the wall of the tower where she'd been imprisoned. But as she pushed, the stilth receded from her touch. Pulling the others behind her, she stepped out of the Way and onto the pebbly bank of the Lake. Her bees, exhausted, settled over her shoulders. Behind her, panting with effort, came the pucks and Phouka. Last of all, the giant spider heaved its way through and crouched wearily beside Rook.

Ready for an attack, she gripped her bow and drew an arrow from the quiver on her back. But no attack came.

The stilth was in the nathe.

The air was heavy and still and the land was stuck in the blurry, gray time between day and night. The cloud-covered sky pressed down on them. All along the edge of the Lake, and spilling out over the grass all the way to the gray wall that surrounded the nathe, were people. Many of them sat huddled around campfires that had gone out, dark, lumpy shapes in the chilly air. Some were hidden away in tents. Others stood watching the Lake with dull eyes.

Her feet crunched loudly on the pebbly bank; the water was absolutely still. She could feel the stilth in the Lake, heavy and waiting. None of the people moved as she stepped closer to them. They didn't even react to the crowd of pucks that lurked behind her.

"Okay," she said softly, and her voice sounded loud in the stuffy air. "Here's what we're going to do. Tatter?"

The healer-puck stepped up beside her. "Here," he said.

"They're wildling," she said, and handed him her

knapsack. "You know what to do?"

"I do, yes," he answered, but he didn't move.

She glanced aside at him. He stood staring out at all the people. The little spider he'd taken as a pet crouched on his shoulder. The stilth, she realized. It was affecting him, too. "Tatter!" she said loudly.

He started, as if waking up. "Right," he answered, and shook his head. His pet spider poked him with its front feelers.

"Try to hurry," she told him. Hurry in the face of something that wanted them all to slow down until they were still and silent. "Be a puck," she said. Be stubborn and snarly and tricky, she meant. "Fight it."

Tatter nodded and, collecting Phouka and another puck with a nod, found a clear area and started unpacking herbs and tinctures from the pack.

She called a few of her bees to her. "Keep an eye on them," she said, pointing to Tatter and the other pucks. "If they start slowing down, do something."

Zmmmmrm, the bees said.

"Yes," she answered. "Sting them if you have to. The spiders should help." Anything to keep the pucks from falling under the influence of the stilth. Now for the next thing. "Rook?"

She heard his feet scuffing over the pebbles. "This is much worse than it was before, Fer," he said, coming to stand beside her with the spider looming behind him. "We don't have much time left."

"I know." She could feel it: the stilth seeping through this land, flowing into the Lake and from there into all the Ways, spreading its stillness and death. "The Forsworn are here, just as we thought. Can you get the spider started?"

Rook looked around. "It's too light here." He nodded toward the gray wall that surrounded the nathe. "Maybe in the forest there's enough darkness."

Leaving a few bees and half of the pucks and Phouka behind to help Tatter with the medicine and the wildling people, Fer led Rook and Asher and Rip and the rest of the pucks to the viney, gray wall. She was a Lady, so it opened under her touch, but slowly, the vines oozing apart to leave a narrow opening that the spider barely squeezed through. The forest beyond was shadowy and dark.

Rook led the spider under the eaves of the trees, where he spoke softly to it. Slowly the spider eased into the darkness; then it squatted and, with its long, spindly back legs, started drawing lengths of shadow-thread from itself; with its front legs it wove the thread into a thick, clotted web that it hung from the trees' branches like heavy curtains.

"Can you see to this?" she asked Rook. "We need

to be sure there's enough web for all the Forsworn, and hopefully for the other Lords and Ladies too."

He shook his head. "You're going into the nathe, aren't you?"

Fer nodded. She had to give the Forsworn one last chance to fulfill their oaths to her. This would be the third time asking, and the most powerful, so she had to try it.

"Then I'm coming with you," Rook said firmly. "Ash can stay here." He turned to the other puck. "Can't you, Brother?"

"I can do that, yes," Asher answered after a long moment.

No, he couldn't; not if he was stuck in the stilth. Fer stepped closer to him and dared to reach up and take his chin so she could look right into his flame-colored eyes. His pet spider scurried to the top of his head and clung there. "Listen, Ash," she said firmly. "The stilth will try to stop you. Don't let it."

He jerked out of her hold, his glare suddenly fierce. "Leave it, Lady," he growled.

"I won't," she growled back. Then she grinned. "Be a puck, okay?"

He barked out a surprised laugh. "Oh, I think I can manage that." He sobered. The spider waved its front feelers at Fer, as if reassuring her. "Take Rip with you to the nathe," Ash said. "He'll keep you out of trouble."

"Get us into trouble, you mean," Fer muttered, but she nodded. She left a few bees behind with Asher. Then, with Rook at her side and Rip a step behind, she headed toward the nathe.

The forest here had always felt ancient, but now the stilth weighed on it so heavily that the trees' heads were bowed and their branches drooped; their leaves hung limp. The trees barely noticed her as she passed, leading Rook and Rip through air as thick as honey, but dry as dust. The three bees she'd kept with her flew lower and lower, as if pressed down by the heavy air. Finally they landed on her shoulder and clung there, buzzing with annoyance. Trudging, she and the pucks emerged from the forest. The wide lawn that lay before the nathe had once been green; now it was gray-brown, the grass shriveled and dead. Across the lawn the nathe itself loomed, its windows empty.

"So this is the nathe, is it?" came Rip's rough voice from behind her.

That's right; he'd never seen it before. Fer nodded.

"It's full of nathe-wardens that hate us pucks," Rook put in. "So watch out."

"I like it," Rip said.

Fer glanced over her shoulder to see that he was grinning. Well, Rip was one puck who never forgot his fierceness; he'd fight the stilth harder than anyone. He was the right puck to come into the nathe with her and Rook.

The nathe. They were almost there. It was time to confront the Forsworn and get them to fulfill their oaths.

🍃 🍃 🍃

With his brother a step behind him, Rook followed Fer over the dry grass and up one of the gnarled stairways that led to one of the many doors into the nathe. She stepped inside, and when he stepped after her he felt as if he'd run headlong into a stone wall—and then gotten stuck in the stone itself. He took a breath. It was like trying to breathe with a weight of rocks on his chest. Then another. Then a blink that took a thousand years. Something felt cold and smooth under his cheek. Somehow he'd ended up sprawled on the floor. All the bruises he'd got from trapping the spider awakened with a yelp.

"Are you okay, Rook?" Fer asked. Her voice sounded very far away.

He started to nod, and then she was by his side, crouching, her eyes full of worry. "You're not moving," she said. She touched his forehead, and time started again, and he dragged in a deep breath. She turned away, and he realized that Rip was on the floor beside him, also caught in the grip of the stilth.

He felt her hand take his, and he let her drag him off the floor. With her other hand, she held Rip. "Hold on," she said. "As long as you stay close to me, you should be okay."

"Okay," he echoed. He heard Rip growl his agreement.

Staying close, he and Rip followed Fer through the silent, dark hallways. At last they reached the nathewyr, the grand hall at the very center of the nathe. Sitting in front of the double doors were Fer's friends Gnar and Lich. They were huddled together with their arms around each other and their heads bowed.

"Hello?" Fer said.

Neither of them moved.

Leaving him and Rip, Fer bent and put a hand to Gnar's dark cheek, and then to Lich's pale one. At her touch, they looked slowly up. Gnar blinked. The usual fires in her eyes were banked, the color of ashy embers. Lich rubbed his face with a heavy hand. "Lady Strange," Gnar croaked, as if she hadn't spoken in a long time.

Fer knelt by their side. "Are you okay?"

Lich spoke as if he was forcing the words out. "It's too late, Lady Gwynnefar."

Gnar shoved at Lich with her shoulder. "Maybe not too late, Dewdrop, now that the Strange One is here, with her pretty puck."

Rook growled at that. Stupid spark-girl.

"The Forsworn are inside?" Fer asked, pointing at the double door.

"They are, Lady," Gnar answered, suddenly solemn.

Fer got to her feet, and then helped Gnar and Lich stand up. She nodded at Rip. "Can you stay with them?"

His brother grinned and gave her a sharp nod.

"Get out of the nathe if you can," she told them. She waved her hand, and one of her three remaining bees flew to Rip, where it hung over his head, buzzing. "And back to the Lake. You go too, Rook."

"The stilth won't get us, Lady," Rip said. He bared his teeth at Gnar and Lich. "Get up, you two." The fire-girl and the swamp-boy climbed to their feet.

Gnar was staring at Rip. "He's got a huge spider on his neck," she said, pointing.

"You think *this* spider is huge?" Rip shot back, grinning. "Come on, fire-girl. I'll show you a real spider." He pushed Gnar and Lich, and holding hands, they started down the hallway.

Before following them, Rip leaned in to whisper into Rook's ear. "You're staying true to the Lady, Pup? Like you said?"

"I am, yes," Rook whispered back. "Go on."

Rip gave a sharp nod and, followed by Fer's bee, went after Gnar and Lich.

Fer had turned to face the double doors of the nathewyr. She took a deep breath, as if steadying herself. "All right," she whispered. "I can do this."

"You can," he told her, even though she hadn't been talking to him.

"Rook," she said, turning to him. "You didn't go." She frowned. "You should have gone with Rip; it's not safe here."

"I'm staying," he said. *Staying true,* he meant.

"Okay," she said, then paused, as if thinking. "Actually, I need you to do something. Go and find the Birch-Lady and bring her here, to the nathewyr." She flicked a finger, and one of her two remaining bees left her shoulder and bumbled through the heavy air to land on his shirt collar, where it buzzed a low greeting. She gave him a quick, sharp grin. "The bee will sting if the stilth starts to get you."

"Oh, sure it will," he grumbled. On his collar, the bee gave a smug buzz.

"Hurry, okay, Rook?" she asked, suddenly serious.

Yes, he would hurry, as fast as the stilth would let him go. He was not leaving Fer to face the Forsworn alone.

twenty-seven

Fer took off her quiver and set her bow at the side of the double doors, then opened them and stepped alone into the nathewyr.

Dazzle.

She blinked and then squinted. Her bee buzzed with alarm. It was blindingly bright inside, like looking into the sun. It made black spots dance in front of her eyes.

And the stilth. The air was so heavy that to breathe she had to suck the air into her chest and then push it out again. She took a step forward, and it was like wading through hip-deep mud. Time had stopped here and then stagnated.

The hall was crowded with Lords and Ladies, all glittering with glamorie. They were not Forsworn, but in coming here to hide they had forsaken their lands and their people, and they'd been caught up in the stilth. They needed to change too, to give up the false rule of the glamories.

The end of the room, on the platform where the High Ones usually sat, was even more dazzling—so blazingly bright, she couldn't even make out any figures.

You are a Lady, she told herself. This false glamorie had no power over her. The room darkened; the glamories faded, and maybe the pucks' ability to see truly had rubbed off on her, because she saw the Lords and Ladies as they really were. Some were bent like gnarled trees; others were pale and faded, almost like ghosts; still others were squat and rough-skinned, like toads. They didn't look beautiful or noble anymore.

All of them were stuck like statues, caught in the grip of the stilth.

"Come on," she whispered to herself, and started toward the platform at the other end of the nathewyr.

The first time she'd been here the Lords and Ladies had stared at her in disgust, and sniffed as if they'd smelled something nasty. *Not a true Lady at all,* they'd whispered. *Part human,* they'd sneered. But now they looked at her differently. Their eyes were wide, and as she passed she felt them trying to pull away, even as the stilth pressed down upon them.

They almost looked . . . frightened.

Well, they should be frightened, Fer figured. Their lands and their people were dying, and they would die too, if the stilth kept spreading.

She stopped and bent to peer at a hunched mole-Lord who had a long, pink nose and a bald, pink head patched with peltlike, black fur. The mole-Lord's eyes were tiny, but Fer saw truly: the Lord *was* afraid.

He was afraid of her.

She straightened, surprised. She wasn't a frightening person. Was she?

Maybe she was. She was a Lady, with all a Lady's power, and she had demanded oaths from other Lords and Ladies—oaths that had been impossible for them to fulfill. She had wanted them to change everything about the way they lived and ruled. When she had come to the nathe before, to demand that they fulfill those oaths, she hadn't been careful, and—as far as they knew—she and the puck she'd brought with her had killed the Birch-Lady. Now she was here again, the only Lady with the power to resist the stilth. They had no power at all compared to her.

No wonder they were frightened.

Don't worry, I won't hurt you, she wanted to tell him, but she knew he wouldn't believe her.

Fer went on faster now, pushing through the stilth to

the blaze of glamorie where the nine remaining Forsworn awaited her on the platform. When she reached it, she stopped and examined them carefully.

Their glamories were desperately bright, like sunlight reflecting from hot metal. And inside . . . it looked like the Forsworn were being stretched out to nothingness by their glamories and by the stilth. They were shriveled and gaunt. Their eyes were wide with terror, and with enmity, too.

"Be careful," she whispered to herself.

Slowly she climbed onto the platform. The pucks, she knew, didn't think much of her plan to talk to the Forsworn. But maybe it wasn't so stupid after all. "What I could see before," she told them, "was your power. But now I see what you really are." The Forsworn were shriveled, bitter, malevolent creatures, clinging to their power with trembling claws, terrified of any change. She stepped closer. When she continued, her voice rang out through the nathewyr. "I ask you a third time to fulfill your oaths to me and take off your glamories."

One of the Forsworn Ladies gave a wail of rage; two other Ladies gripped each other's hands; the rest cowered.

The Sea-Lord—their leader, Fer realized—scuttled a sideways step closer to Fer. His seaweed hair hung dry and limp from his head, and he was hunched into himself.

"We cannot remove the glamories," said the Sea-Lord. His eyes narrowed and Fer caught a malevolent glint. "The fault lies just as much with you, Lady, as it does with us. You should never have demanded such an oath."

For just a second, Fer felt a tingling of regret. "It's true," she admitted, "that I didn't think through the consequences of asking you to swear an oath to me." She went on, growing more sure of herself. "But I was right to ask you to take the glamories off. The glamories make power too important. You don't need them to be connected to your land and people. Even now it's not too late to make things right." She bent to look into the Sea-Lord's eyes. "We brought a shadow-spider with us. If you step through its web, the glamories will be removed. All you have to do is step through. That's all."

The Sea-Lord shrank away from her, and the other Forsworn hissed with dismay. "No, Lady," he spat. "The web will kill us, as it killed Marharren."

"She seeks our deaths!" the Forsworn Lady wailed.

"No, the Birch-Lady is alive," Fer explained. And she could prove it. Where was Rook? She turned and peered through the brilliance of the nathewyr. There—a dark blot against the brightness. Rook was standing in the doorway of the hall, not moving. Another dark shape stood beside him. "Come with me," Fer ordered.

The Sea-Lord nodded, but edged around her. The

other Forsworn followed, and she led the shuffling group through the Lords and Ladies to the door of the nathewyr, where Rook and the Birch-Lady waited. The other Lords and Ladies gathered behind them, moving slowly like stone statues come to life.

Fer stepped past the Birch-Lady to stand beside Rook. He had a reddening bump on his neck where her bee had stung him. "All right?" she asked.

Rook gave her a slow nod. "She's been hiding in Old Scrawny's room. He's coming too."

Arenthiel? She nodded. "Good." She touched Rook's hand to keep him out of the stilth, then looked at the cluster of Forsworn and at the other Lords and Ladies, and pointed at the Birch-Lady. "See?" she asked them. "She's not dead."

The Birch-Lady stepped forward to meet them. Like an ancient birch tree, she was gnarled, with gray patches at her knobby elbows and knees and a fall of withered, leaflike hair hanging over her face. She had dark eyes set into the mass of wrinkled, barklike skin. She was ancient, but she wasn't ugly. She gave the gathered Forsworn a brisk nod. "Listen to the girl, you fools. She is right about the glamories. When my glamorie was gone, the puck told me to go back to my land and my people, and so I did. The stilth had been strong there, and the people needed me. But with my oath fulfilled, the stilth was leaving my land, and I could help them." She pointed at Rook. "Let the puck touch you with his cursed hand, as he touched me," she said. "It is painful, and you may die of it, but your oath will be fulfilled."

Beside her, Fer felt Rook give a start. He raised his web-smudged hand. "I promised I wouldn't," he said. "You can't use me to be rid of the glamories."

Fer knew that Rook was right. The Forsworn couldn't put it on Rook to take their glamories away. "We have the spider outside," she told them. "If you step through its web, your glamories will be destroyed."

"It seems you have left us with no choice," croaked the Sea-Lord. A spark of malevolence still gleamed in his eyes.

"Your choice is that." Fer pointed toward the door leading outside to where the spider was waiting. "Or death. For everyone in all the lands. Eventually the stilth will come for you, too."

The Forsworn trembled at this. Two of the Ladies started to weep.

The Birch-Lady spoke. "Look around you." She swept her arms wide, showing them the nathewyr, the silent, still Lords and Ladies gathered behind them. "Our broken oaths have caused this. The glamories have ruled us for too long. Take the glamories off, and you will be free of them forever."

The Birch-Lady had a different kind of power now, Fer realized. Maybe, now that she'd lost her glamorie, she'd given up rule and . . . she'd become wise.

"Come with me," Fer told the Forsworn. "The stilth is still spreading, and we have to hurry."

For a long moment the Forsworn hesitated. Fer watched carefully, and she saw the spark of resistance in the Sea-Lord's eyes go out. He understood what they were facing.

As fast as she could, Fer led them through the nathe, and shuffling, creeping, limping, they followed, and so did all the other Lords and Ladies, dragging under the burden of their glamories. And the stilth came with them. They passed across the lawn, and then through the forest to the gray, viney wall. There the pucks were waiting.

And so was the spider.

Rook stayed close beside Fer. Staying true, yes, but the stilth surrounding the Forsworn was so thick that it would grip him if he strayed too far.

At the nathe's viney wall, his brothers Asher and Tatter came out to meet them. They had bee stings on their necks too, he saw—Fer's bees keeping them from the grip of the stilth. Rip was there too, with Gnar and Lich.

"Lady," Tatter said with a nod to Fer. "The people are cured of their wildling. But the stilth in the Lake is going to make them sick again if we don't do something soon."

Rook glanced at Fer. Beside the gaunt, cringing Forsworn, she looked tall and strong and wild. "All right," she said firmly. She turned to Ash. "And the shadow-web?"

Ash grinned. "There's enough."

"Well done," she approved. To Rook's surprise, Asher nodded at that, as if her approval was something he actually wanted. Fer turned to him. "Rook, can you ask the spider to spin even more web, for all the Lords and Ladies?"

"I can, yes," he answered. He gave a low whistle, and the spider lurched out of the shadows at the edge of the forest. At the sight of it, the Forsworn shrank away, trembling. "It's not going to eat you," he muttered. Stupid Forsworn. Purring, the spider loomed over him; it reached out with a furred feeler and patted him on the head. He stumbled. "We need more web," he told it.

The spider scuttled to the edge of the forest and started spinning. Its web took shape quickly; a curtain of dark shadows draped from the low-hanging branches. Finished, the spider backed away.

The cluster of Forsworn stared at the shadow-web. None of them moved.

Even in the still forest, the web wavered. It looked like a puddle of darkness hanging in the air. To step through it might be to step through into dark emptiness, or into death.

"The stilth is the death of us all," Fer told them. "You can stop it by fulfilling your oaths."

"The Lady is right," the Birch-Lady put in. "Be brave, as I was not. Our people need us. Our lands need us. Be true Lords and Ladies."

"You have been asked three times to fulfill your oaths," Fer said to the Forsworn. "What is your answer?"

Rook braced himself, just as he knew his brothers were doing, fingering the shifter-tooth in his pocket. If the Forsworn refused to step through the web, there would be a fight.

"We will fulfill the oaths," the Sea-Lord said suddenly. Crabwise, he edged up to the shadow-web. Rook saw him close his eyes, and then he plunged through the web.

Rook held his breath, expecting the shrieks and moans that the Birch-Lady had made when he'd stripped the glamorie from her with his web-smudged hand.

But the Sea-Lord stepped through the other side of the web. The false glare of the glamorie had been stripped away, and he stood on shaky legs, blinking at the pucks and other Forsworn. He still looked like an ancient crab, and he wasn't beautiful or lordly. But he looked solid in a way he hadn't before. To Rook's eyes, he looked *right*.

The choice. Fer had been right to let them choose.

One by one, watched carefully by the pucks, the Forsworn stepped through the web and came out the other side without their glamories. They blinked, as if looking at the world through new eyes. The two Ladies who had been weeping clung to each other, and they were still weeping, but now they shed tears of happiness.

"They're free," Fer said from beside him. "I didn't realize before. They hated the glamories, even while they were wearing them."

"Arenthiel told me they were slaves of the glamories," Rook remembered. "I guess they really were."

She smiled up at him. "They've fulfilled their oaths, Rook. That means we've defeated the stilth."

"It does," he answered, grinning back at her. He'd helped with it too, and so had his brothers. Soon he could tell her about staying true, and she'd believe him, and all would be well again.

After all the other Lords and Ladies had stepped through the web and been freed of their glamories, Rook followed Fer and the newly freed Forsworn through the opening in the viney wall to the pebbled edge of the Lake of All Ways. There, the crowd of waiting people stood silently watching. Plump seal-people and mole-people, and a couple of mouse-boys, and fern-girls, and the proud skunk-girl and her friends. People from all the lands. They had been cured of the wildling; they could see that their Lords and Ladies were no longer wearing their glamories. Everything had changed.

"Hello," Fer greeted them, smiling.

They didn't answer. The air was heavy.

Too heavy.

The bee on Rook's collar gave a shrill buzz. He tried turning his head to look at it, but he couldn't move. Out of the corner of his eyes he saw the Forsworn and the other Lords and Ladies huddled together, unmoving. On the other side, his brothers stood still and silent, Fer's bees buzzing frantically around them.

A step ahead, Fer turned to face him, her eyes wide.

Behind her, the Lake's surface turned sooty black— as black and blank as any night without stars or moon. Black tendrils seeped from it, creeping along the ground. Whatever they touched shriveled and died.

Fer, watch out! he wanted to shout, but his words were stuck in his throat.

Her bees howled around her, and she whirled to face the Lake. She saw it.

The stilth. It had gathered its strength in the Lake, and now it was coming for all of them.

It was too late, Rook knew. The stilth had won.

twenty-eight

Fer staggered back. The Lake of All Ways seethed and bubbled; coils of shadow seeped from it.

The Forsworn had fulfilled their oaths; the Lords and Ladies had removed their glamories; everything had changed. But, Fer realized, it hadn't been enough.

Her heart pounding with sudden fright, she took another step back from the Lake. Beside her, Rook stood with his head lowered, caught in the stilth. Everyone was caught; she was the only one who could move. The heavy air pressed against her; every breath was a struggle.

What could she *do*? They were all going to die—she had to do something!

Her bees settled around her in a cloud, as if protecting her.

"The stilth is in the Lake," she realized. It was in all the Ways. It was everywhere. The stillness and death of changelessness.

Never forget that you are human, her grandma had told her once. And she had never, ever forgotten it. Being human meant she made changes happen. She herself was change. She remembered how the stilth in the Lake of All Ways had pulled away from her. From her human-ness.

She took a step toward the Lake, and her shoulder brushed Rook's.

At her touch he stirred. He drew a ragged breath. Then, "Fer, what are you doing?"

With a shock of cold, she realized what she had to do. "I'm going into the Lake to fight the stilth," she answered. Into all the Ways, all at the same time. "It's the only way to stop it." She was about to take another heavy step toward the Lake when she felt Rook's hand seize hers. He stepped up beside her. "What are you doing?" she asked.

"What's it look like?" he answered. His face was pale and set. "I'm coming with you."

She shook her head. "Rook—" Her voice faltered, and she took a steadying breath. "It's going to be danger-ous. We might not be able to come back."

"I know that," he said. His hand gripped hers more tightly.

"You can't come," she insisted. The air had thickened even more, and darkness was rising up all around them.

Rook's yellow eyes glared at her. "I won't let you face this alone, Fer. I'm staying true to you, all right?"

Staying true? He'd told her what that meant to a puck. "Rook, you can't," she whispered.

"Leave it," he growled. "Let's just get this over with."

She nodded. They were beyond friendship now. "Thank you." She squeezed his hand, and turned with him to face the Lake.

Her breath sounded harsh in the silent, heavy air. One breath, then another. One step, then another. The grate of pebbles under her feet. Rook's warm hand around hers.

Slowly she bent and, using her Lady's power, she opened all the Ways. She stood. The stilth rushed around them, a silent roar. Rook's lips moved, but she couldn't hear his words. It was time. She and Rook started to step into the stilth-filled Lake.

Then, from behind them, a voice rang out like a trumpet—*"Wait!"*

She cast a quick glance over her shoulder.

The sky was black and the land was wrapped in the dread silence of the stilth. But light was coming. Like beacons in the darkness, the High Ones strode, with Arenthiel hobbling by their side. The stilth parted around them like black fog; they glided past the Forsworn and the Lords and Ladies and the pucks and all the people who were balanced on the very precipice of death. They came to stand before Fer and Rook at the edge of the Lake of All Ways.

The two High Ones looked as calm as ever; their faces were still and lovely—but they were weary, too, as if they were using the last of their waning power. "Lady Gwynnefar," one said in her musical voice; they both bowed their heads in greeting.

All Fer could do was stare back at them.

Beside them, wizened, old Arenthiel gave Fer a grin and a sideways, hidden wave. "Lady Fer," he said. "And the young puck with her. I knew you would stay true, dear Rook."

Fer gave Rook a quick, astonished glance. He was *friends* with Arenthiel?

As an answer, Rook shrugged.

"Lady Gwynnefar," one of the High Ones repeated. "We three come to help drive back the stilth."

Fer found her voice. "It's too late," she explained. "I have to go into the Lake to fight it. I'm part-human. I understand why it has to be me."

"No, it does not," the High One said. "For too long we have resisted change. Here, now, we embrace the change you bring to us, Gwynnefar. And you show us now why we must no longer trust to oaths to bind us together."

Fer nodded. From the very start she had known that oaths were wrong.

"But we cannot be unbound from one another," said the other High One. "What shall bind us instead, Gwynnefar?"

Fer asked herself the question. What bound people together? It wasn't a hard question, but it was one only her human self could answer. "Love," she said simply, because it was a simple, human answer.

At the sound of her voice, the people and the Forsworn and the Lords and Ladies stirred.

In the Lake, the stilth continued to churn; its deathly, black smoke towered over their heads and spread across the sky.

Love, Fer thought. Love for her people and her land— the same love shared by all the people here. "We don't have to do this alone," she said to Rook, and raised her hand that was holding his so that all the people could see it. Then she turned and offered her other hand to one of the High Ones. With a wan smile, the High One took her hand. The other took Rook's hand, and then came Arenthiel, and then all the people and the Lords and Ladies were linking hands along the banks of the Lake.

Against them, the stilth roared and swirled.

Fer felt her human half so strongly. She *was* caught up in a river of time, hurtling along, days slipping past like seconds. At the same time she felt how love transcended

Grand County Middle School
MEDIA CENTER
Moab, Utah 84532

time, how it was stronger and deeper than any oath. She felt her connection to her land and the people, and to all the people standing on the bank of the Lake.

Together they were a wall against the stilth. It battered against them like a huge wave—powerful, deadly—and stalwartly they flung it back again. The tendrils of stilth retreated to the lake. It gathered its strength for one last, battering rush; Fer felt its heavy, crushing weight and darkness, and against it she called up her love for her land and for all her people, for Twig and Fray and for Phouka's wildness and for the pucks laughing around the fire, and Grand-Jane's comforting embrace, and most of all she called on Rook staying true to her, on the steady warmth of his hand in hers.

The stilth shrank back. Its black tendrils drew in until only a writhing cloud of darkness swirled at the center of the Lake. It hovered there, contained but not defeated.

Fer found that she was panting for breath; beside her, Rook looked pale and weary, but he'd fought hard too; he'd had his tie with his brothers and with her to draw on. Along the edge of the Lake, the other Lords and Ladies and all the people were trembling and leaning against one another for support.

The two High Ones and Arenthiel—three High Ones—stood together. All three seemed dim, as if a light within them had gone out. Arenthiel gave an exhausted, rattling cough that shook his frail body; the other High Ones bent over him like drooping flowers.

"Are you all right?" Fer asked, worried, keeping an eye on the last of the stilth in the Lake. She had her knapsack full of herbs and medicines; she could make them a healing tea if they needed it.

One of the High Ones shook her head. With a frail hand she pointed at the remaining stilth that hovered in silence at the center of the Lake. "It waits for us," she said wearily. "We have ruled here for too long, Gwynnefar. The nathe has been a place outside of time, without change. Now change has come and our time here is over."

"Wait," Fer gasped. What was the High One saying, exactly? "You can't—"

"The change will be hard for everyone," interrupted the other High One.

"Will these lands fade?" the first High One put in. "Will the people die out? Or will they change and love and thrive? It is up to you, Gwynnefar. Will you help them?"

She nodded, suddenly understanding what had to happen. "I will," she promised sadly.

"And you, too, Rook," Arenthiel added.

"I will, Old Scrawny," Rook said, his voice rough.

"Well, then!" Arenthiel said, and, leaning on the

other High Ones, he turned away.

Slowly the three High Ones paced to the Lake, where all the Ways stood open. They reached up, and like pulling curtains of darkness after them, gathered the remaining stilth into themselves. Calmly they stepped into the Lake, and the stilth swept after them like the hem of a long dress. The darkness receded. The three High Ones went away—into all the Ways—and they were gone.

twenty-nine

Fer found herself crying against Rook's shoulder. His arms were wrapped around her. She cried for the brave High Ones and Arenthiel, gone forever, and for the sudden release of all of her exhaustion and fear. The tears kept coming.

"You're getting my shirt all wet," came Rook's grumpy voice.

She gulped down another sob. "Sorry," she said with a watery sniff. She looked up.

The sun shone down, warm on her shoulders. Her bees buzzed happily overhead, golden-bright against the blue, late-afternoon sky. She heard the quiet lap and rush of the Lake's waves on the pebbled shore.

She stepped away from Rook and rubbed the tears off

her face. All around them, the people, free of the stilth, were stretching, smiling, looking at the world with wondering eyes. Several were gathered around the Lords or Ladies who had once been Forsworn. There were hugs, and more tears, and barks of joy from the seal-people as they found the Sea-Lord.

She took a deep, steadying breath, and then waded into their midst. The High Ones had given her a job to do, and she would do it. "Listen, you people," she shouted. But there were too many of them, and they were too excited.

Then, a ripple in the crowd, and Phouka pushed through to her. He shook his head and snorted. "Good idea," she said to him, and grabbed his mane, pulling herself onto his back. "Hey!" she shouted, and now all the people could see her and hear her. After a few moments they quieted, listening. She caught the Sea-Lord's eye, and nodded at him and at the other formerly forsworn Lords and Ladies. "Your lands have been poisoned by the stilth," she said loudly. "It's gone now, but the lands won't recover so easily. You'll have to go back."

She saw heads nodding. The people stirred.

"But here's the thing," she said, holding up her hand so they'd wait to hear the rest. "The glamories are gone. There will be no more rule. You will have to work together to heal the lands."

"We belong to the land, Lady," the Sea-Lord said with dignity. "We remember now. We can do this."

"We can!" others shouted.

"The Ways are clear of the stilth," Fer told them. "You can go now, and get started."

There was a surge toward the shore of the Lake, and the Ways started opening as all the Lords and Ladies led their people back to their stilth-stricken lands.

Phouka pranced as people pushed past him.

"Thank you, Lady," called the Birch-Lady, surrounded by her saplinglike people. They hurried to the Way, eager to return to the Birchlands.

Fer nodded and then sighed. All the lands had been damaged by the stilth. She thought of the Sealands, the horror of the plain of mud, and the forest land draped in the cocoons of dead butterflies. Fixing those lands would not be easy. They had a lot of work ahead of them.

And oh, she was tired. Wearily she slipped from Phouka's back.

"And what about us, Lady?" Asher asked. He gave her a glinting grin. All the pucks, including Rook, stood behind him in a shifty, dark crowd, watching her. "Got anything for us to do?"

"Ha," she answered. As if she'd order the pucks around.

"We've decided, Lady," Rip answered. He stood with

hands on hips, his yellow eyes fierce in his black-painted face.

"We have, that," Asher added. "We pucks are tired of wandering around all the lands, having no place to call our own. We like the nathe, and this handy Lake of All Ways, and now that the High Ones are gone, we're going to live here."

She opened her mouth to protest.

The pucks watched, waiting to see what she would say.

She swallowed a giggle. Pucks at the nathe! Living with the nathe-wardens! It was perfect, really.

Laughing, the pucks gathered around her. Phouka nudged her shoulder.

Hm, yes. She had something to settle with Rook. She reached out and grabbed his arm and pulled him out of their midst.

The pucks made a circle around them. Rook watched her warily.

She smiled back at him and felt a bubble of happiness floating inside her. "Well, pucks. There's something else. Your brother Rook has stayed true to me."

They laughed at that. "Leave it," Rook growled at them.

She smiled at him, then stepped closer. "And I will always stay true to you, Rook," she said, holding out her hand.

He took it and nodded, suddenly solemn. "You are true, yes." The pucks stilled around them.

"Do you know what this means, Lady?" Asher asked, from the circle of pucks.

"I do, yes," she answered.

"If one is true, it means we're all true, Fer," Rook said to her.

She nodded. It meant she was one of the pucks. They were bound together. She could *feel* the bond with them, feel it in her heart. It was stronger than promises, stronger than friendship, stronger than oaths.

She looked around at the pucks. Tricksy, all of them. Black hair, flame-colored eyes, full of trouble. Her brothers. "So I'm a puck now, am I?" she asked.

"You are, yes," Rook said warily.

She grinned up at him. "Okay. So when do I get to turn into a horse?"

The pucks stared.

"Or a dog?" she asked. "You've all got a shifter-tooth, right? Don't I get a shifter-tooth, too?"

"You do, Fer," Rook answered, smiling at last. "You do, yes."

She laughed. Being one of the pucks was going to be so much fun.

But she was never, ever going to eat any rabbits.

acknowledgments

Thanks to:

My editor, Antonia Markiet, who is a freaking genius. And to associate editor Rachel Abrams and editorial assistant Abbe Goldberg.

My agent, Caitlin Blasdell, and Liza and Havis Dawson at the Liza Dawson Associates agency.

To the wonderful publishing team at HarperCollins: publisher Susan Katz, editor-in-chief Kate Jackson, editorial director Pheobe Yeh, senior production editor Kathryn Silsand, copy editor Kara Levy, senior art director Amy Ryan, senior designer Tom Forget, production manager Shayna Ramos, associate publicist Olivia DeLeon, and cover artist Jason Chan.

To my first readers and dear friends Deb Coates, Greg

van Eekhout, and Jenn Reese.

To the Blue Heaven crew for helping me survive yet another exciting medical emergency, especially Charlie Finlay, Rae Carson, Toby Buckell, and Cassie Alexander.

To Jessie Stickgold-Sarah for making Fer a better rock climber.

To my wild animal children, Maud and Theo, and to my dashing mad-scientist husband, John.

Don't miss a moment of this enchanting fantasy-adventure series.

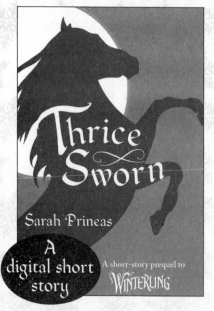

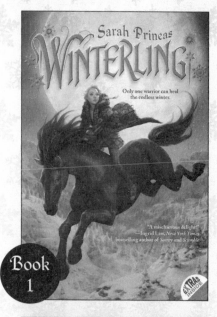

HARPER
An Imprint of HarperCollinsPublishers

www.harpercollinschildrens.com

More from
SARAH PRINEAS

The
MAGIC THIEF

Where cities run on living magic and
a thief can become a wizard

HARPER
An Imprint of HarperCollins*Publishers*

www.harpercollinschildrens.com

Grand County Middle Schoc.
MEDIA CENTER
Moab, Utah 84532